Adventures of a
COUNTRYSIDE
DOCTOR

Dr. Thomas T Thomas

Adventures
of a
Countryside Doctor

Dr Thomas T Thomas

Cover design by Ranjit Jose

The cover painting is done by the author himself.

DEDICATION

This book is dedicated to my parents,

The Rev. T. Thomas

and

The Late Mrs. Annamma Thomas.

CONTENTS

ACKNOWLEDGMENTS

I acknowledge with extreme gratitude…,

My whole family for the support and encouragement- especially my wife, **Dr. Annie George** who tolerated my much reduced involvement in the kitchen.

The Editors – my cousin **Ms. Molly Kurian**, my sister-in-law **Ms. Achamma Mathew**, and my daughter **Ms. Anu T. Thomas.** Without their close scrutiny, this book would have had gross timeline errors!

Ms. Liliana Gandeva, my dear friend from Bulgaria, who gave regular inputs even on my crude first draft.

My mentors – **Mr. Som Bathla** who gave me clear guidance on writing, publishing and launching,

         Ms. Sweta Samota, who hand-held me throughout the journey. Without her, this book would not have been half as interesting.

Mr. Ranjit Jose, my author friend, who worked on my painting to produce the beautiful book cover.

Mr. Kevin Hill, whose YouTube videos (Paint with Kevin Hill- The Forest River) helped me do the cover picture on my own.

All my friends and former class mates who have always supported me in all my endeavors.

1. An Unwanted Birth on Christmas Night

“**Y**ou mean to say that there is nothing wrong with him, Doctor?!”
The young man's face was contorted with dismay and anguish as he confronted me. Not the sort of reaction one would expect from someone who had just been informed that his wife has just given birth to a healthy, beautiful boy.

“Are you sure? Isn't he premature?” I dismissed the fleeting thought of lying to him. I knew damned well it would be futile.

It was a cold night on Christmas – 1987. Rather, it was the early hours of the next day. I was in Chittar, a remote village nestling among the hilly forests near the southeastern border of Kerala. In those days, the majority of the pilgrims walking barefoot to the famed Sabarimala temple passed through this village. I was working in a mission hospital there, bearing the fancy title of Medical Superintendent. Fancy because there were only two doctors, the other being my wife, Dr. Jessy.

Chittar was starting to develop as a township. There was a private bus connecting it with Ranny and Pathanamthitta, which had two trips a day- one in the morning, and the other late in the evening. Telephone was a luxury, and only those who were very well off had one. It was useful to connect within Chittar, but if you needed to contact anyone outside, you had to book with the telephone exchange for a Trunk Call, which may get connected within eight to ten hours if you are lucky. If it was something urgent, you could book for a Lightning Call which would cost a bomb, but often, it would take several hours for the lightning to strike. Electricity was available in and around the town area, but when a thunderstorm struck, it would be disrupted for days on end. We could keep abreast of the happenings in the outside world by subscribing to a daily. Each morning, by ten o'clock, the previous day's newspaper would be delivered promptly.

I had just started to doze off, after having been rudely awakened by the noisy arrival of a caroling group. They had sung two songs, wholly out of pitch, each one in the group seemingly rendering his separate version of the song. In the end, they asked and collected twenty rupees from me, as an additional punishment for listening to their cacophony. I couldn't help recollecting the beautiful carols we, a group of six youngsters used to render at the homes of the elderly without collecting any reward, while I was a student at the Trivandrum Medical College.

Woken up again by the sound of a loud jeep pulling over at the hospital nearby, I rolled over trying to catch a quick snooze before that inevitable knock on my door. Chackochan, our night watchman cum peon, would soon come to fetch me. A faithful, simple, elderly man, he would escort me the short distance to the hospital shining his heavy torch along the path. More than once, it was his timely warning shout that prevented me from trampling on a snake slithering among the weeds.

The knock, when it came, was loud and frantic. Realizing it to be an emergency, I jumped out of bed and rushed to the door. "New patient.

Girl seven months pregnant, but she is in severe pain." Years on the job has made Chackochan capable of reporting precisely and to the point. I quickly changed into trousers and a T-shirt and rushed after him.

"Call from the hospital" I shouted to Jessy who had just woken up. Night calls were my responsibility. Besides, it would do her good to have undisturbed rest at least at night. Last week, we had found out that she is now pregnant with our second child. Aju, our two-year-old son, was sound asleep.

Briskly walking behind Chackochan, I got to thinking through all the possibilities. Foremost in my mind was preterm labor. How will I manage the child? I hoped they will be affluent enough to take her to a hospital with the proper facilities. The nearest town where a pediatrician would be available was thirty-five kilometers away, but it will take an hour and a half on that apology of a road. There was every possibility that they might be further referred to Thiruvalla, another thirty kilometers away, where neonatal ICU facilities would be available.

Most probably, the relatives will insist on managing the child here itself, citing their poor finances. About a year ago, we had succeeded in saving a premature child weighing just 1.2 kilograms, managed in our own makeshift neonatal ICU with an improvised incubator consisting of a crib with bottles of warm water kept all-around under the felt clothes. But such luck may not always last. I hoped it could be some other manageable cause- like a urinary tract infection. Could it be appendicitis? Another ominous possibility was an ectopic pregnancy, but I dismissed it as unlikely to present itself so late in pregnancy.

I reached the labor room. The silence was intriguing. It was a very young, beautiful lady- Sally, 19 years, as entered in the case file. She was obviously in pain. Teeth clenched, she lay tightly clasping the sides of the large wooden table that served as our labor cot. I quickly inspected the abdomen and was puzzled by its size. The uterus was way too large for a seven-month-old fetus. Could it be twins? As I carefully palpated her abdomen, I couldn't make out multiple limbs as usual in a twin pregnancy. I put on a pair of gloves and proceeded to the vaginal examination. The membrane was already ruptured, and the amniotic fluid was flowing freely. I could feel clearly the full head and the thick tuft of hair on the crown. How could this be a premature child?

"When did you have your last periods?" I asked Sally.

"I don't remember the exact date doctor." Sally seemed to be avoiding my eyes. "I did not have any since my marriage, and even before that, my periods were quite irregular."

"How long have you been married?"

"Seven months, Doctor."

"Now see, Sally, this does not look to be a premature child. Have you, by any chance, had any pre-marital sexual contact?"

Sally now looked at me. Tears welled up in her eyes. She burst into a sob. "Yes Doctor," she answered softly, again looking away.

"Was it your husband?"

"No..." Sally took her time to respond.

"Who was it then?" It was Sister Alice with the demanding question.

I thought of intercepting to spare the girl from such questioning at this stage, but Sally was forthright now and started recounting the story in between the bouts of pain which were now coming at shorter intervals. She spoke as if confessing before a priest.

I had assessed the actual delivery to be more than an hour away. I could have gone back home for some more sleep before they call me once the case became "full" (that's what they say to mean that the baby is about to come out), but I decided to stay back and listen to the story. Besides, how could I answer the questions which were sure to come from her husband and relatives waiting just outside? I asked for a chair to be brought in and sat down.

It turned out to be the tale of an innocent, naive girl, whose present predicament was firmly linked to the happenings on a day about ten months ago in Trivandrum, the capital city of Kerala.

2. Sally's Story

Sally had gone to her uncle's place in Trivandrum with Appa and Amma, her father and mother. She was quite excited about the trip. Life had been pretty much boring for the past three years ever since she barely managed to scrape through her SSLC exam after the 10th standard. Neither she nor her parents evinced any interest in further studies or seeking a job. She spent her time helping her mother with the household chores and reading romantic love stories and sleazy weeklies, of which there were plenty in Malayalam. Houses around the neighborhood subscribed to different weeklies so that they could exchange and get to read all of them.

While roaming the neighborhood for the weeklies, she would sometimes get from her friends what they called "small books". These were the local porn magazines with explicit sex stories. Some would have smeared up pictures of couples in the weirdest of positions. Of recent, Sally had been having dreams full of sex fantasies.

"Uppaapan (that's what she called her uncle) has some plans for you. He has written to me to visit them for a couple of days, and specifically to bring you along." That was all the information she got from Appa.

Sally felt overawed by the tall buildings and the heavy traffic in the city. Uppaapan's house was in a suburb on the outskirts. It was a small but neat house, with polished cemented floor and a concrete roof- a far cry from her house in Chittar with its thatched roof and a floor made of cow dung.

Uppaapan welcomed them heartily as they arrived by evening. "You seem to have really grown up!" he remarked to Sally. Aunty served them tea and snacks- the sort of which they had never ever seen, let alone tasted in Chittar.

"Now Sally, I want you to go out and buy yourself a nice sari." Her uncle counted out two hundred rupees and handed it to her. "There is a textile shop less than a kilometer away, on the right."

"I'll go with her", Appa said, but uncle held him back. "She is a grown-up girl. Let her do it herself. Besides, we have matters to discuss."

Sally felt glad that she had come alone. The sales boys at the shop were all good looking guys, and she had been elated by all the attention she got from them. She could barely contain her excitement as one of them draped the sari on her to assess the match with her skin tone.

While returning home after her purchase, she noticed a huge lorry with an all India number plate parked by the side, on a lonely stretch of road. Suddenly, the door of the lorry opened, and a very tall, fair, handsome bearded man jumped out just in front of her. He was wearing a bright red turban on his head. She jumped back startled.

"Did I scare you?" He asked in Hindi, smiling. Sally just had a basic knowledge of the lingo which she had studied as a second language in school, but she could make out what he said. She shook her head, giggling shyly.

"I am from Chandigarh," he went on. "I will be going back by tomorrow evening. I sleep inside the lorry itself. It's really cold!"

They continued talking- he in Hindi and she in Malayalam both just understanding just a little bit of each other. She felt that they could go on forever, but then she came back to her senses. "I have to go now, bye..." Reluctantly, Sally continued on her way. She saw him blowing her a kiss. She didn't feel bold enough to return it. She gave a parting wave, instead.

Amma was not too pleased with her purchase. "This sari looks too loud. It won't be suitable for the occasion we have in mind." Sally had purchased a bright orange-red sari which she had chosen after considerable thought.

"There was another one I liked, and I knew you would too, but that was two hundred and forty. I didn't have that much cash."

"Get that one then." Uppaapan counted out fifty rupees and gave it to her. "You can go tomorrow. Don't lose the bill. They will readily exchange."

That night, sleeping on the soft mattress, Sally again had her fantasy dreams. The scenes were intimate and passionate, and the man was the truck driver.

The next day after breakfast, Sally set out again to the textile shop. She found herself wishing that she would come across the truck driver. She spotted the lorry still parked at the same spot. She looked around, but he was nowhere in sight.

There was not much delay in the shop as she knew which sari to buy. Her pulse started racing as she saw the driver standing by the side of the lorry while returning.

"Hi!" She was the first one to greet. The lorry driver too seemed glad to see her. They started talking like long lost friends meeting again.

"I will be leaving for Chandigarh in a few hours. My colleague will be joining me from Kollam. We eat, rest, and sleep inside the lorry itself, most of the time."

"Do you have space inside to sleep?"

Soon, he was helping her into the cabin to show her where he had spread his bedding. One thing led to another, and by the time she scrambled out of the lorry and hurried back home with a parting wave, she was feeling a painful, yet pleasurable sensation in her loins.

Realizing she was quite late, she quickened her steps. The image of the handsome lorry driver passed through her mind and brought a smile to her lips. "Should at least have asked him his name," she thought. Sally was panting heavily by the time she reached her uncle's house. Everyone was out, sitting on the knee walls of the verandah, looking out for her.

"What took you so long?" Her mother demanded, scanning her face. "Why are you so breathless? What happened?"

Sally had her answer ready. On her way back, she had noticed several stray dogs. Some had even come up to her, sniffing her ankles. Ordinarily, she would have stooped down and petted them, but she had shooed them away.

"I was surrounded and chased by dogs!"

"But you are so fond of dogs." Her mother's voice had a ring of suspicion. "And where is the sari you went to buy?"

Sally realized with shock that she had left the parcel in the lorry! Her mind raced for a plausible explanation. "One of the dogs snatched it and ran off. I chased it, but I fell down and it got away!" she blurted out.

"Those dogs might have mistaken it to be a food parcel," Uppaapan opined. "These municipality people have no sense of responsibility. These stray dogs are breeding and multiplying like...like...er, like dogs!" He fumed with righteous indignation.

"It seems you have hurt yourself," Appa held her arm to show a long scratch below the elbow. Somewhat deep, it had tiny drops of blood trickling out. Sally remembered the sharp, searing pain she had felt during their frantic lovemaking in the lorry. She hadn't even looked to see what it was. It might have been some protruding screw.

"Come, let's wash it clean." Amma took her to the washbasin and vigorously washed the wound with soap and water. "There is not much dirt. Anyway you have to take a shot of TT. But when can we do it? Tomorrow will be super busy. Come now. We have to discuss something important."

Everyone had gathered around. Appa and uncle were seated on two out of the three chairs available. Amma, Aunty, and Sally sat on the floor. All eyes seemed to be on her.

Uppaapan opened the conversation. "Do you know why I sent you out to buy a new sari? A boy is coming to see you tomorrow."

Sally gaped in disbelief. "Aiyo! Not now, please."

"What? Didn't you agree just last week that we will start looking for a suitable alliance for you?" There was a tinge of annoyance in Amma's voice.

It was true. Amma had spoken to her about marriage. She had been only too eager then. For a fleeting moment, the image of the handsome lorry driver flashed through her mind. But she didn't even know his name! Probably he was married. Should be- he looked to be in his forties. Maybe he will present the sari she had left in the lorry to his wife. Anyhow, it was highly unlikely that their paths would cross again.

"Okay then," she sighed in resignation.

"Good!" Her uncle was enthusiastic. "But what will you wear? The sari you bought is lost. I don't want you to meet your future husband wearing old clothes. The boy and his family will come tomorrow morning at ten."

"I bought a new churidar for Mini last week. Let's see if it will suit Sally." Mini was Uppaapan's younger daughter. She was an engineering student, staying in a hostel in Kochi.

Sally was trying on a churidar for the first time. Just two years back, she had graduated from the above-knee short skirts to the long ones. It was a sari for all formal occasions. The red churidar clung to her body a bit too tight. It brought to focus what her friends used to tease her, as 'disproportionate assets'. She felt sexy and beautiful.

The boy was not bad looking. They had come noisily announcing their arrival in their family-owned jeep. Johnykutty- that was his name- sat fidgeting shyly opposite Uppaapan. Eleven people had come all packed into that rugged vehicle. A few plastic chairs had been taken on rent and all the men were seated. The ladies stood crowded at the back. Sally and Amma were in the kitchen preparing tea for the guests. The Halwa was cut into smaller pieces. They had prepared vada at home itself, getting up early. These were served together with some spicy mixture.

All eyes were on her as Sally went around serving the tea. As she bent down to offer the cup to Johnykutty, their gazes locked for a few seconds. She felt him staring at her as if enraptured by her looks.

"This alliance will work out", Uppaapan said after they left, pointing towards the empty plate in which the halwa had been kept. "When the boy's party prefers to take the sweet snacks, it means that they liked the girl", uncle replied to Sally's puzzled look.

3. Sally's Story Continued

The marriage was fixed to be held on the 25th of March- exactly three months later. It was a modest function by local standards. There were just about a hundred guests. The feast was simple- just fish curry and fried chicken as the non-veg. dishes, and just two desserts. Throughout the ceremony, Sally's mind was on the fact that she had not had her monthly periods in the last three months. She feared whether she could be pregnant but hoped fervently that it was not. She wanted badly to discuss her fear with close friends, but none of them were reachable. Most of them were already married off to distant places.

The wedding day went off like a whirlwind. They made a short visit to the bridegroom's house, straight from the wedding. Sally was escorted into the house by her mother-in-law holding her by the right hand with a lighted bronze oil lamp in the other. Sally took care to put her right foot in first while entering her future home. Two cups of milk were brought in for the bride and groom and glasses of fresh lime juice for the rest.

It was then time for them to leave for Sally's home in Chittar, with Appa and Amma. The first night was to be at the girl's house before the couple return for good the next day.

It was nearing eleven when they were finally alone in their bedroom. The bed was bedecked with rose petals and jasmine flowers, giving out a sweet fragrance. Sally came in with a glass of milk. Johnykutty had a few sips and passed the glass for Sally to have the rest. Both had not spoken a word. There was palpable anxiety in both of them. Sally had a nagging fear that Johnnykutty might realize she was not a virgin and reject her outright. Johnnykutty was worried about other things. It was the first time he was alone in a room with a lady other than his mother.

"Shall we have a bath and get ready for bed?" Johnnykutty finally broke the silence. "I'll go first".

He grabbed his multi-colored lungi and a T-shirt and rushed to the bathroom outside. Pulling away the white embroidered Jubba soaked wet with sweat, he proceeded to have a quick bath. He regretted not having given heed to those friends who had advised him to have a swig of brandy soon after the wedding, so as to handle this first night with confidence. He thought he would somehow avoid sex that day. He was feeling anxious and too tired for anything.

Returning from the bathroom, Johnnykutty was shocked to see Sally had already started changing from her wedding dress. Her ornaments were all neatly stacked on the table and she was unwinding her sari.

The sight of her standing there in just her skirt and blouse evoked in him feelings he never knew had existed with such intensity before. He could feel all tiredness and nervousness leaving him, and testosterone taking over. He quickly crossed across and holding her in a tight hug, pulled her onto the bed.

Sally watched fondly as her husband fell into an exhausted sleep. If at all he had realized that she was no virgin, he certainly gave no inkling to that effect. She was amused by his high passion and clumsy act. The lorry driver seemed such a professional. "This is the boy for me," she thought. "I must get that lorry driver off my head."

The following months brought days of bliss. Her husband and in-laws were nice to her. The only dampener was the recurring thought about the baby growing within her. She could feel the changes. She deliberately pushed out such thoughts from her mind, thinking she would face it when the time comes.

Everybody was so happy about her pregnancy. There had been a celebration of sorts at home when she and Johnykutty came home that day from Pathanamthitta holding like a treasure a small plastic card on which two red lines were very clearly visible, confirming her pregnancy.

Her mother-in-law occasionally remarked how big her tummy seemed. "It might be a very large baby. Wonder if you will have a normal delivery- otherwise we will have to go to Pathanamthitta for a caesarian". The poor lady never did think of any other possibility, though enough of ominous hints were dropped in occasionally by the neighbors.

4. Sally Leaves Hospital

Sally started straining really hard. The head of the child popped out facing down. I waited patiently for it to turn ninety degrees and face sideways, along with the natural rotation of the baby. 'Watchful expectancy and masterly inactivity'- our gynecology teacher in medical school used to repeatedly quote from the textbook. Once the baby had turned fully, I eased out the upper shoulder pulling the head down. Then I got the lower shoulder out by changing the direction of pull upwards. The rest of the baby came out easily and I held it high, holding it aloft by the legs, like a trophy. The baby let out a loud wail, announcing his arrival to the world. (Yes, it was a male).

Those waiting outside were unlikely to have missed the full-throated cry. It was a perfect textbook delivery- one of the most gratifying moments in a doctor's life.

I watched Sally's face smiling with happiness and relief, change quickly to one of apprehension. "What will you tell them, Doctor? Can you please tell them that the baby is premature?"

"How can I?" I asked helplessly. "The baby is fully grown and mature, as anyone can see."

****

"Are you sure Doctor?" That was Johnykutty again. "But we have been married for just seven months!"

I confirmed the maturity aspect impassively. "Shall I ask them to bring the baby for you all to see?"

"No!" It was his father with the emphatic reply. "We don't want to see him. In fact, we are now leaving. You can do whatever with that girl and her child."

Something snapped in my mind. *What will I do if they just leave?* I drew myself up to my full height. "You brought her here and it is your responsibility. If you just dump her and leave, I have no option other than to call the police. You will then have to follow it up from there."

His father paused as the full significance of my words sank in. He called the others together for a huddled discussion. I left them at it and went back to check on the mother and child.

"They don't want to see the baby," I told Sally. I could see something like the last flicker of hope leaving her face. She burst into violent sobs. My heart went out to this young girl. I comforted her, patting her on the back. "I am sure everything will work out okay."

I could hear a two-wheeler starting up outside and moving away. Anyway, the jeep in which they had come was still parked outside. I got the nurse to open the consultation room. Walking past the small crowd with a grim face, I went in and sat down. Normally I would be happily walking back home now, having conducted a completely normal delivery- with both mother and baby fine. *What will happen to this young girl and her child?*

It has been more than a year since I had been stuck in this godforsaken place. It was entirely my father's fault. Even as a child, he had cleverly implanted in my immature mind, the ludicrous idea that earning money is least important. Being a doctor had been my ambition, but his advice was- 'Become a doctor and go serve in a place where there are no medical facilities. Don't worry about money. Your life will be fulfilling and your children will flourish'. He used to say that with such conviction, that I fell for it.

It was not that I did not enjoy the demanding life here. But I was not free to go anywhere, other than shuttling between hospital and home. Too busy while at the hospital to think about anything else and fully engaged by my son's antics while at home expecting Chackochan to arrive any time with another call from the hospital, I was literally on duty twenty four hours. Each day brought its own challenges.

I had not been a particularly studious student at medical school. (Maybe that is an understatement) My father once had confronted me with a report he had received from one of my lecturers, who also happened to be a relative. "Your son puts in so little effort at studies. He is intelligent enough to get through with this, but if he puts in some more effort, he can score high and earn a post-graduate seat for specialization."

"What will I do with specialization if I am going to work in a remote area with not much medical facilities? As a specialist in a particular subject, how will I manage the common cases there?" My father was stumped by this answer and this enabled me to continue my happy-go-lucky routine within the campus.

It was free for all in the men's hostels of the college. We were free to come and go any time we chose, and we made the most of it. But I made sure to attend the clinics regularly and tried to acquire enough skills needed for working independently in a rural setup.

I was jolted back from my thoughts by a commotion outside. I could make out Johnykutty's father arguing loudly. The answering voice was subdued and defensive. The interaction was brief, and soon there was a knock on my door. It was Johnykutty's father with another middle-aged man looking all dejected and forlorn.

"This is that girl's father. He will be responsible from now on. Our duty is over. We are leaving."

"Wait!" I shouted and turned to Sally's father. "Do you agree that you will take full responsibility?" He nodded in agreement. "Okay," I said to Johnykutty and father. "You can leave if you wish."

"Come!" He ordered his son and stormed out with never a backward glance. Johnykutty followed him meekly. I noticed his eyes fleeting to the direction of the labor room where Sally was lying. He seemed to be in great turmoil.

"Where is my daughter?" implored Sally's dad soon as they walked out. I led him to the labor room. He rushed across and held his daughter in a tight hug, both sobbing unashamedly. We could now hear the loud noise of the jeep starting and moving away. The noise got fainter and fainter and the stillness of the night took over.

Sally and the baby could be discharged by the third day. The hospital stay was uneventful. She appeared melancholic all day. Mostly all the nurses were sympathetic, except for Sr. Alice. She could never forgive Sally's horrible sin.

On the day of discharge, Sally's father walked into the consultation room. "Doctor, our bill has come to four hundred and twenty rupees. I know you don't charge high, but all this happened unexpectedly. I can manage to pay only three hundred now. I promise to come back within two weeks and pay the rest." I sighed inside. This was a common occurrence. Experience has shown that only one-third of such cases return. "Okay, but please be sure."

I ordered the staff to prepare for their discharge. "Next person," I told the sister manning the OP.

"Shoukath Ali!" called out the sister. I kept seeing patients one by one, my wife doing the same at the other table. "Sally and family are leaving," Sister announced to me sometime later. I excused myself from the patient I was examining and went to see them off.

Sally came to me. "Thank you for everything, Doctor. Please pray for me... and the child."

"Sure," I said and repeated to her for the umpteenth time- "Everything will somehow work out okay, Sally". I wondered if I sounded convincing enough.

Her parents had already started walking out. I later came to know that they had walked all six kilometers to their house, as they could not afford to hire a jeep.

Little did I realize then how much I would get to be involved in their future affairs.

5. Chittar Mission Hospital

The hospital was owned by one among the numerous Christian church denominations existing in Kerala- the same that I belonged to, by default.

We had our pre-appointment interview at Kottayam, with Rt. Rev. Dr. Zacharias Mar Coorilos, Bishop of the Diocese which owned the hospital. I had heard of him as being a very learned, pragmatic, and unassuming man.

The Vicar of the local church in Chittar, and President of the local committee for the administration of the hospital, introduced us to the bishop. "Thirumeni, this is the doctor couple who have come forward willingly to work in our Chittar Mission Hospital."

'Thirumeni' – meaning His Holiness, was how bishops were addressed and referred to. In our denomination, bishops were chosen from among those priests who managed to remain unmarried till their middle age. Having a good, long beard was an added qualification.

Those who got selected even without a beard were expected to grow one before the coronation. They were given fancy new names. Culex Mar Anopheles, Monkey Mar Rhinoceros, etc. were some fun names we used to cook up as kids.

Zacharias Thirumeni was a short, somewhat stout bishop in reddish-brown simple cotton robes, his hair covered with a black headdress adorned with small gold-colored crosses, like a veil. He was just past middle age, and his beard had only started greying. He had a kindly face. I immediately took a liking to him.

Thirumeni gave us a benevolent smile. "You will be doing immense service to the local community, Doctor. Your service will be appreciated by all."

"But will people really benefit? We will have to charge them for our services. Can people there afford it?"

"We will give concession and free treatment to those who need it," Thirumeni replied.

"But who will decide which patients will get to benefit?"

"Of course the local committee!" The Vicar intervened.

"But can the local committee meet and decide for each case? I don't know who all are the people going to be on the committee. Will they be impartial? Won't they come up with demands for concessions to undeserving people?" I was skeptical.

Thirumeni paused for just a second. He turned to the Vicar. "The Medical Superintendent shall decide," he said decisively.

I had a few more issues to bring up. "I've heard that the hospital is lacking in even basic facilities. We have to improve on it if our work is to be meaningful."

Thirumeni thought for a while. "Some members of the Diocesan Council have actually opposed the reopening of the hospital because we have had to dole out money every time the hospital got into working mode. We don't expect anything from there, other than that the hospital runs smoothly enough so that we won't have to support it financially. I can't immediately allow for additional investment. If it functions without interruptions, I am sure the hospital will be able to build up enough funds. I will help as much as I can. I'll use my influence in the council to sanction necessary funds." He blessed us with a prayer, and we took leave.

We set out for Chittar by the evening of a pleasant day in June 1987 in a hired taxi from Thiruvalla with Aju, Jessy, and her parents. My in-laws were coming particularly to see where this crazy doctor of a son-in-law was taking their daughter. The furniture we had and my Suzuki bike had been taken there in a tempo van in the morning by my father, who was waiting there for us.

It seemed a long journey. After an hour's drive, we reached a place known as 'Boundary'. It was the place from where, just forty-five years ago, the evergreen stretch of the Periyar forests began. The road almost ended, and we started the slow, bumpy ride through a tract that had been tarred once, maybe a decade earlier. If a vehicle chanced to come in the opposite direction, one of them would have to back up to someplace with enough space for the automobiles to cross.

"This road is not meant for a car". The driver muttered irritably.

He might be raising the stakes to demand a higher fare. But he was right. We had not seen any other car on the way- only jeeps with people jam-packed inside, as well as hanging out from the back. Sometimes, there were two or three men on the bonnet too!

We seemed to be leaving civilization behind us. Small houses cropped up now and then, with patches of banana, tapioca, and other vegetables around them. These were people who had encroached into the forest and set up their living there. The government back then would give title deeds to whoever cleared the land for agriculture.

There were no buildings now, and we were passing through an undisturbed forest area. The trees were thick and heavily canopied.

Occasionally, we caught sight of monkeys swinging from tree to tree. I took in deep breaths to savor the fresh and pure air.

The forest area gave way to rubber estates and then scattered small shops, as we neared the 'town' where the hospital was located. The doctor's quarters was just about a hundred meters away. My father was waiting there, having got the entire luggage unpacked and the furniture set up in each room.

Leaving everyone at the doctor's quarters to set up the house, I walked to the hospital where the staff had been told to assemble.

Mathai Sir, the longest-serving veteran member in the local committee, and the Vicar were there to introduce me to the staff.

All the staff members seemed to be in a happy mood. They had been out of work and without salary for the past many months. Most of them were struggling to make ends meet, and they looked forward to the reopening of the hospital with great expectation.

Not so Lissy, the lab technician. She was financially comfortable- her husband, also a lab technician (albeit a qualified one) was working in a large hospital in Kuwait. She was not a qualified technician, but had learned some techniques from a private lab in Pathanamthitta from where she had some training and earned a certificate.

Sister Mariamma was the senior-most. Then there was Alice, Moncy, Sabeena and Veena. Kochumol was in charge of the pharmacy. She confided to me that she had actually trained to be a nurse, but ended up in the pharmacy. Then there was Chackochan and his wife Mary Chedathi, who was the sweeper. Five other girls had come hoping to be accepted as trainees.

The ward and the rooms had been cleaned up and fresh sheets had been spread out on the beds. I stepped into the Pharmacy and inspected a few of the medicines stacked on the racks. Many of them were past the expiry date. "Why are you keeping all these here? Sort out all the medicines now and throw out all those whose dates have expired", I ordered Kochumol.

I next went to inspect the lab. It was a small cramped room. There was a microscope, a centrifuge, some bottles filled with reagents, and a stack of test tubes. There seems to be a lot of upgrading to be done here. *When will we be able to transform this into a proper Hospital?*

While having dinner together, I apprised everyone about the present state of the hospital. "It's just not enough, restarting it- we have to upgrade it to such an extent that people won't have to travel to Pathanamthitta, except for advanced treatments."

I thought I saw an appreciative glint in my father's eyes.

6. First Day in Chittar

We arrived early in the morning to start the first day's work at the reopened hospital. There was a crowd already waiting. As I and Jessy made our way through the crowd, we found the veranda occupied by the vicar and other committee members. "This will be our program for the reopening," the Vicar said and showed me a scrap of paper.

"What is this? A public meeting?" I pointed to the stack of files on the consultation table. "There are patients waiting!"

"It will take just a few minutes, Doctor", quipped Mathai Sir. "We have to celebrate this historic moment."

I had noticed a young boy among the crowd who seemed to have trouble breathing. "No way!" I was emphatic. "We can't keep patients waiting." I turned to the Vicar. "Please say a short prayer, and then, we will start the OP. The committee members were visibly upset. They had all come prepared for the felicitation speeches.

The prayer was not exactly short. He took around fifteen minutes- basically reminding God about the history of the hospital, the foresight of the founding bishop, the sacrifices of the local people- especially Mathai Sir, to keep it running, how it had been plagued by frequent disruptions, etc. He finally ended with thanks to the marvelous doctor couple who have now made possible its reopening and a fervent plea for His Grace to bless the hospital to flourish henceforth, and for all eternity.

"Amen!" I shouted loudly at the end. "Now call in the patients- that boy first". I pointed to the boy having breathing difficulty who seemed to have become worse.

"See you all later. Now we are starting our work," I said to the Vicar and committee members who seemed about to follow me back into the consultation room.

The boy was almost breathless. He had already been to a quack and received two injections in the early hours of the day. "Take him to the ward and start him on oxygen," I ordered. I proceeded to treat him as a case of 'status asthmaticus'- as I have seen being done in medical college. I wrote down a prescription for a cocktail of drugs to be given through an intravenous line at ten drops per minute and called in the next patient.

It was a young girl with scabies all over her body. I wondered how she had tolerated this highly irritable and itching lesion all these days. Then there was an old man with uncontrolled diabetes and a deep dirty ulcer on his leg. It went on thus, without a break. Jessy was seeing patients at the other table. I got up in between to check how the boy with asthma was doing.

The boy was as breathless as before- if not worse. They had not connected the oxygen. The infusion of medicines was going way too slow. I blew my top. "What's this?!" Why is he not getting the oxygen? And what good will these infusions do at this rate of flow?" I shouted, while adjusting the drip myself.

"It's been a long time since we used the oxygen, doctor. We were not able to open it". Sister Mariamma was apologetic.

"Why the hell didn't you tell me earlier?" I was getting really irritated. I tried opening the valve of the cylinder with the spanner but it was stuck tight. Seeing me struggling, Chackochan rushed in with a heavy log of firewood from the kitchen. With one sweep, he hit the spanner. It was like Chris Gayle hitting a six. There was a loud 'POP' and a forceful hissing sound along with the sound of glass breaking. The cylinder had been opened all right, the oxygen rushing out with such force that the tubes got disconnected. Chackochan's blow had also broken the glass flow-meter and the humidifier- the glass container with water through which the oxygen was supposed to bubble.

Turning the spanner back, I adjusted the flow and connected the nasal cannula directly from the cylinder to the boy's nose. Fortunately, we had another glass bottle to which the rubber cork with the glass tubes of the humidifier would fit. Soon, we could get humidified oxygen at a reasonable rate of flow.

I decided that I should end once and for all, such sloppy responses to my instructions. I turned to Sr. Mariamma. "Once the staff for the night shift also arrives, I want all of you to come and meet me in the consultation room. We will be having a meeting".

****

It took another couple of months to set the house (rather, the hospital) in order. The boy with asthma on that day was the first inpatient. The number of outpatients as well as inpatients kept increasing day by day. In two months, there were always ten to fifteen inpatients every day. Fifteen was the total number of beds available.

There were two storerooms with lots of old files and broken equipment.

We got them cleared and purchased two new beds to be put in them, so that the bed strength of the hospital now rose to seventeen.

The hospital was now running at full flow, and around seventy patients were coming daily for consultation. The inpatient beds also were almost always full. Eighteen deliveries had been conducted successfully, all with no problems to either mother or child.

It was at this time that the Vicar approached me. "Thirumeni is coming for a visit this Sunday evening. We have to convene the local committee that day at your quarters". It was to be a day of high drama, which forever changed my approach to patients.

On that day, I realized that I will have to exercise more care while handling patients.

7. A Terrible Tragedy

It was the first local committee meeting since the reopening of the hospital. Thirumeni himself was coming all the way from Kottayam. The meeting was to be held in my quarters. Tea and snacks were arranged. Just before his arrival, there came a call from the hospital. Molly, who had been coming regularly for antenatal checkups, had arrived with pains.

Jessy went to attend the delivery, leaving me with our son and the committee members, waiting for Thirumeni to arrive. Being a Sunday, it was the maid's day off.

The white Ambassador car with Thirumeni arrived at my gate. He came directly to me with an extended arm and gave a warm handshake.

"I'm so glad to hear that you are performing exceedingly well here, Doctor. All credit to you".

"Thank you..."

Before I could continue, Chackochan came up and interrupted our conversation. "There is some problem with the delivery case at the hospital. Dr. Jessy asked me to call you."

"I'll just go see what it is and come back soon," I told them and turned to Chackochan. "Please stay here and keep an eye on Aju".

I could sense something amiss as soon as I entered the Labour room. "The baby's head is engaged and fixed but just not coming out", Jessy said.

"Have you tried the vacuum?" I asked.

"Not yet. I was thinking whether to".

"Okay, I will take over. Aju is there at home with Chackochen. Thirumeni and all the committee members are there. You can serve them tea and tell them I will be coming shortly".

As soon as Jessy left, I asked them to get the vacuum extractor ready. Smearing lubricant gel on the suction cup of the instrument, I kept it on the baby's head. I nodded to the sister to start pumping out air.

We had a crude vacuum extractor. It was basically a large glass bottle with an airtight cork having two glass outlet tubes. One outlet is connected to the suction cup applied to the head of the baby and the other to a hand pump much like a small cycle pump. I expected a mild CPD (cephalo-pelvic disproportion- pertaining to the circumference of the baby's head and that of the pelvic outlet) but hoped she would deliver with the help of the vacuum. I started applying steady traction to the head but it would not budge. I increased the force of my pull but the cup came off with a loud pop.

Frustrated, I looked at my watch. It must have been more than half an hour since Thirumeni arrived. I wondered if they had started the meeting. There were many important things I wanted to discuss.

"We will try again", I declared and braced myself for the next attempt. This time I felt a slight movement, but again the suction cup came off with another horrifying pop. My heart raced. I listened for the fetal heart with my stethoscope and thought it had slowed down.

"Again", I called out. "Raise the negative pressure to 600 mm!" That was the maximum pressure allowed. It failed the third time too. I was feeling exhausted. It seemed futile to refer the patient at this stage for a caesarian. The fetus was already showing signs of distress. I tried once more and failed. Finally, I got the baby out at the fifth attempt. Anxiously, I waited for the first cry from the baby. I gave a sharp slap on its buttocks, but the child just lay flaccid. I checked for its heartbeat. There was just a feeble, slow beat. We started frantic efforts to save the baby. After some time, I realized it was futile. The baby was dead.

"Sorry", I told Molly. "We could not save the baby".

Tears rolled down her cheeks, but she was quiet and accepting. Watching our frantic efforts, she had guessed something to be seriously wrong.

I walked out of the labor room. "We have lost the baby", I told the small crowd of her relatives outside. I went and sat in the consulting room. *It's entirely my fault. Maybe if I had referred them early enough for a caesarian, the baby could have been saved. In any case, there was no justification for me to repeatedly try the vacuum extraction! It might have caused some internal damage to the brain.* 'Watchful expectancy and masterly inactivity'- I seemed to have grossly ignored this dictum. It was the impending committee meeting that had made me act the way I did.

Through the window, I could see Thirumeni coming out of my house and getting into his car. As it drove past, I could see him looking out towards the hospital, from the back seat. Some of the committee members were walking towards the hospital.

I recognized their familiar voices talking to Molly's father. "There was some serious cardiac problem with the child", one of them declared unambiguously. "There was no way he could have survived even if he had been taken to Medical College".

Mathai Sir came into my room. "We have told them that the baby was having a severe heart disease. You can stick to that".

The half-door opened again, and 5-6 people came in. "What exactly happened, Doctor?"

"Frankly, I don't know", I answered in a broken voice. I could not control the tears swelling up in my eyes and freely rolling down my face. "I think the baby could have been saved if she had been referred to someplace earlier for a caesarian." From the corner of my eye, I could see Mathai Sir quietly leaving the room.

Molly's father came over and put his hand on my shoulder. "Please don't be upset, Doctor. It is God's will". My fault or God's will? He continued to comfort me. "We know you did your best, Doctor. Continue your good work. We will pray for you".

I considered myself an agnostic. I rarely visited the church. But in a way, God was responsible for saving me from condemnation on that day. I could only marvel at the goodness of these people. Or is it because of their blind belief in God and fate? What if they were atheists? Would they have responded in a different way? I concluded that atheist, agnostic, or believer; it is the basic nature of each individual that makes them behave the way they do.

Molly was admitted for the day with IV fluids. She was exhausted by all the effort. Her father approached me with a request. "Doctor, since the baby was stillborn, we don't bury him in the church. Even if born alive, there is no religious burial for anyone who has not received baptism. Can we bury him in the hospital compound?" There was a stretch of land behind the hospital building, within the compound itself. Overruling dissenting voices from some of the committee members, I granted permission.

"Doctor, it won't be proper to allow them to bury the child in our compound without the sanction from Thirumeni, or at least the local committee," Mathai Sir pointed out to me.

"I will take responsibility." I stood firm. Chackochan helped them with the burial.

I went home with a heavy heart. Not being in the mood, I asked my wife to attend the next call from the hospital and sat down on the floor with my son. He was full of playful antics, but it only brought me more memories of the dead baby. Who will now opt for delivery at our hospital? If at all someone comes, will I be able to handle it?"

Just then, Chackochan appeared and announced that another labor case had come and my wife was busy with several other patients. Leaving Aju again with Chackochan, I walked again to the hospital.

This was Sreekumari, who had been coming regularly for checkups. She was tall and a well-built, healthy lady. I anticipated no problems. This was her second pregnancy. Her three-year-old child also had come with her grandparents, eagerly waiting for the arrival of the younger one. Brushing away all negative thoughts, I proceeded to the task at hand. It was a perfectly normal delivery. The boy was crying his heart out.

I went to check on Molly before returning home. "She was alright but started crying after she heard the cry of the baby just born," Sister told me.

As I walked back home I felt my confidence returning. There is nothing more fulfilling for a doctor than conducting a normal delivery and seeing the smile of fulfillment on the mother's face upon hearing the cry of the child.

I learned later that the committee was wound up without transacting any business, due to the absence of the Medical Superintendent. Thirumeni had insisted that no decisions be taken in my absence.

A few days later, I received a letter from him. He had written not to be disheartened by the setback and to go ahead and plan to develop the hospital. 'I understand it is difficult for you if you are to get clearance from the local committee for everything. I am giving you the freedom to make decisions as required. I will support you.'

8. Sally Gets Discount

Two weeks after Sally had left home with her parents and her son, her father turned up. "I have come with the balance money that I owe to the hospital, Doctor."

"You can pay it at the counter," I said. As he went out, I remembered them trudging home on foot with the child after being discharged from the hospital, as they could not afford to hire a jeep. Don't they deserve some charity?

There always had been controversies about my decisions regarding the sanctioning of free treatments. Many in the local committee were displeased about the absolute powers given to me by Thirumeni in this aspect. I took great care to see that this was given to truly deserving patients. I relied on my assessment from the appearance and dress but sometimes was often misled.

An elderly man once came in. He had a slight stoop, and was bare-chested, with just a towel slung over his shoulder. He had problems of high blood pressure, cholesterol, and sugar. He produced an old prescription from a physician in Pathanamthitta. "I had been going to this doctor for a check-up regularly. But times are hard and it is difficult for me now. I hope you will check me and adjust my medicines. And please give me the maximum deduction on the bill."

I promised I would look into it, and sent him to the lab to get the investigations done. I called in Sr. Mariamma to find out if she knew him and whether he deserved some concessions. Sister could not hide her amusement. "Doctor, he is one of the richest men in Chittar. He deals with cashew nuts which he purchases from the small farmers. He has about thirty people working for him to process and pack the nuts and send them for export. Don't be fooled by his appearance. He never wears a shirt, except when going to church."

I felt foolish. *Appearances can be deceptive!* "Okay let him come. I will deal with him."

Another day, a well-dressed elderly man was brought with a high fever and difficulty in breathing. He had all the accompanying morbidities like diabetes and high blood pressure. He was diagnosed to have acute pneumonia and was admitted and intensive treatment started. They opted for the best room we had- one of the only two bath-attached single rooms. After five days, he was better and ready to be discharged.

He came to my room just before discharge. "Doctor, I am an evangelist of the church. I am eligible for free treatment or at least a very significant discount."

I was taken aback. "We don't give discounts to those who use the rooms. It is only for those patients admitted in the wards," I informed him.

"You don't know me, Doctor. I will get Thirumeni himself to direct you." He was arrogant.

"You do what you want, but you are not leaving without settling the bill." I was not one to be intimidated and made that clear to him.

"Okay then, we will wait for tomorrow," he replied and went back to his room.

By the evening of the next day, he settled the hospital bill in full and left without a word. I came to know that he had sent a messenger to Kottayam to see Thirumeni. He was sent back with instructions to settle the bill at the hospital and if he wants any financial support, to give an application to the church.

Sometime later another controversy arose- this time about being too generous. A beggar woman had come with her eleven-year-old son. She looked old for her age. Her younger child, a girl of around seven years was also in tow.

The boy looked like a football! His mother narrated how he had progressively developed swelling in the legs and the face, till the whole body was swollen.

I asked about his urine output and the mother replied that he was barely passing urine in the past few days. I checked his blood pressure which was way too high. He had marks on both legs from skin infections. Pus was oozing from some of the ulcers.

When asked about this, she told me how this had been there for over a month, and he was taking treatment from an Ayurveda doctor who supposedly was giving medicines to expel all the pus. Though the boy was swelling up and having a fever, she seemed happy that all the pus was being pushed out!

Acute nephritis! I was sure about the diagnosis. It must have been caused by the skin infection. The body fights against the infection with antibodies, and all the dead bodies from this fierce battle get piled up in the kidneys, blocking its tubules. The kidneys get inflamed and fail in their duty of excreting urine. All the fluid accumulated in the body, making it swell up.

The boy was admitted to the ward. The diagnosis was confirmed by lab tests. Treatment was started- totally avoiding salt, restricting fluids, daily monitoring of urine output and weight, and six-hourly injections of Crystalline Penicillin. On the first day, Lasix was also given to help the kidneys flush out more urine. He started improving.

Mathai Sir 'happened' to drop in a few days later. "I heard there is a beggar woman with her child admitted here. Will they be able to pay our bill?"

"We will give them a maximum discount," I replied.

"You will have all the beggars coming here! Better send them to a government hospital." He went on in a sinister voice. "The members of the local committee are not too happy with your decisions. They say that you are giving concessions to tramps and beggars while refusing it to evangelists of the church."

I did not heed his advice. The boy was improving day by day, his weight came down by more than five kilograms, the swelling had subsided, and he was looking more like a human. He had to be in the hospital for more than a week. Before discharge, the bill book was brought to me. I wrote down the bill for each item. Having been in the ward, his bill was relatively low but still came to 240 rupees. How much discount should I give? I figured them to be too poor to pay anything. Without much hesitation I wrote the discounted amount as 240 and the balance to be paid- 'zero.'

Before leaving, the lady came in with her children. "I will pray for you daily, Doctor. You and your children will be blessed," she said with folded hands. Her voice had the strong ring of sincerity and conviction that left a lasting effect in my mind. It seemed to echo the words of my father while persuading me to work in a remote place. It became a habit for me even years later, to recall her words whenever I had a feeling of being down and challenged.

I called Sally's father back. "Wait! I think I can write it off. Do sit down now and tell me how Sally and her son are doing."

"Thank you so much, Doctor." He seemed visibly relieved as he sat down. "Actually we are going through a really tough time. Sally just sits and broods all the time. She hardly takes any food. She takes care of the child, but her breast milk has dried up and we have to buy formula foods to feed him. It's a real strain on our finances. Our neighbor has a cow that yields plenty, but they are reluctant to sell us milk. We have been isolated by everyone. People are even reluctant to talk to us, though I know they are talking a lot about us behind our backs. It was with great difficulty that I put together this money to clear our dues here. Now that you have let me keep it, we will at least have enough to buy milk powder for the child for a couple of weeks more."

He seemed happy to have found someone willing to listen to his troubles. I could see that even he had changed a lot. He had lost weight, and his face looked haggard. "Tell Sally to come and see me someday," I advised. "Let me see if I can talk to her and try to relieve her depression."

"Next week, we are planning to go to Kasargod. We all need to be away from this place for some time. My cousin stays there. She had been very close to Sally. We were not having much contact with her since she got married and moved to Kasargod- the place is so far off from here.

"Ever since this incident, she has been writing frequently asking us to visit her. She wants us to stay with them for a month. Her husband is a very nice fellow, and they are relatively well to do. It will be a welcome change for us."

I agreed. "I will see you after you return from Kasargod, I said, and bid him goodbye. "Give Sally my regards."

9. A Friend in Chittar

Getting to know CKM was one of the best things that happened to me while at Chittar. CKM was C. Kurien Mathew, proprietor, salesman, cashier, and everybody else at CKM Agencies- the small, but only hardware shop in Chittar. I had gone there to get some tools and nails to fix some hooks and hang up some pictures at home. After getting the things and paying the bill, I was about to leave when he stopped me.

"Please wait a minute. I haven't seen you before. May I know who you are?"

I introduced myself. "So you are the new doctor!" He seemed overjoyed to meet me. "Why don't you please sit and have a cup of tea before you leave? I would like to know you better."

"Sorry, but you know, I am always on duty. You can't know when the next call will come from the hospital. It will be too bad if they can't find me."

"Don't worry doctor," he said pointing to the telephone on his table. "Just call the hospital and give them this number. Ask them to call if needed."

It was one of the very few telephone connections in Chittar, another one being at the hospital. I called the hospital and asked them to call back for a confirmation. I felt relaxed and comfortable. It was the first time I was away from the hospital and home without having to worry about not being reachable in case of an emergency. CKM rang a bell, and his son of around twelve, appeared. "Ask mother for some tea for both of us. This is the new doctor."

His wife was smiling as she brought in the tea with some cutlets. "We are so pleased to have you here! We now have someplace to go in case of any medical problem, God forbid!"

As I sat munching on the cutlets and sipping tea, I noticed the photograph of a middle-aged man displayed under the glass on the tabletop.

"Your father?"

"This is Dr. K .M. Thomas. He is God to me!"

Noticing my raised eyebrows, he went on to explain.

"While working in an American company in Saudi Arabia as an engineer, I developed pain and swelling in the right thigh, along with high fever. I was admitted in a major hospital there, but was getting worse day by day. The doctors decided that the only way to save my life was to amputate the right leg, down from the upper thigh. I flatly refused, and decided to come back home to try treatment here. Many friends advised me against taking the risk. I was being treated at one of the best hospitals in the country, and the company was paying for my treatment."

A friend had recommended Dr. K. M. Thomas, an orthopaedician in Kochi. By the time he reached the doctor's hospital, he was delirious with fever. His right leg was red, and swollen to double its size.

"I'd rather die than get amputated," CKM told him.

The doctor was kind and empathetic. "There is no way I am going to amputate your leg now. I will plan for a surgery by which I will remove all the pus and debris and then see if the antibiotics work."

He had to stay in the hospital for three weeks. The surgery had left a large crater on the side of his upper thigh. Dressings were applied daily, and new flesh started growing slowly. The skin started to grow and cover the wound. By the time he was discharged, he could walk with the aid of crutches.

"That is why he is God to me," CKM concluded. "With the gratuity amount I received from the company and the savings I had, I bought this old house and built a shop in front, and started this hardware business. Though the income is just a fraction of what I was earning in Saudi, I am surviving and still having both my legs! Once in a while, I get pain and swelling. I will immediately contact Dr. Thomas. He will prescribe some medicines, and it will subside."

The phone rang. It was for me. The aged diabetic patient admitted in room four was running a high temperature and seemed to be delirious.

"We will meet again!" I shouted and rushed to my bike.

"Your purchase, doctor." CKM ran after me and handed me the parcel I had forgotten. I noticed he had a slight limp.

Visiting CKM became almost a daily routine. I would take a nap after lunch. The calls from the hospital during that time were attended to by Jessy, giving me undisturbed rest, enough to energize me to attend all the night calls. Most of the child births happened at night. 'What started at night will end at night,' our Professor in Gynecology would say.

Invigorated by the nap and a cup of coffee, I would start the evening OP by three-thirty. Jessy would also join in a little later. Having together seen the patients already waiting, I will leave. Aju will be dressed up and eagerly waiting to get on the bike. CKM's children would be eager to engage him.

I would sit with him in the shop, talking about everything under the sun. Occasional customers would drop in and he would attend to them, while I sat watching. By the time my wife finished OP and came back home, I would also be back with Aju.

This daily break from routine helped fill in the void of the camaraderie I used to have with my friends in Trivandrum. Jessy did not have the luxury of any outside contacts. On rare occasions, she made a visit to her parents with Aju. She would take the Saturday evening bus, to return by evening the next day. It was a tiring journey but gave her some relief from the monotony.

Occasionally CKM would invite us to join them for lunch on Sundays. All of us enjoyed the occasions- not just for the camaraderie and fellowship, but the lavish and sumptuous food laid out for us.

10. A Villain Within

There was no dearth of patients. But by the month-end, after I had paid everybody, including myself, my wife and all the staff their salaries, and cleared the electricity and other bills, there would be very little left as savings.

I had been counting on saving some amount each month and build up a fund to develop the hospital. I made a thorough analysis of income and expenditures. The major income was from the sale of medicines and the largest expenditure was also medicine purchases. I could see that the little margin we got from the sales was gone in transportation costs.

It was Mathai Sir who was in charge of drug purchases. I confronted him one day. "Sir, we are not making any profits despite having so many patients. Most of our income is from the sale of medicines but we are not getting any margin for that."

"I get the supplies from a wholesale drug dealer- St. Mathew's Drug

House, in Ranni. Those guys are a stinky lot. They won't reduce the price, even though I bargain hard with them." Mathai Sir sounded a little bit defensive.

"Next time, I will go myself and try."

He was not very enthusiastic. "It will be a waste of your time, Doctor. Besides, it will affect the work at the hospital."

"Dr. Jessy will manage alone for one day," I replied. "Anyway, I want to try."

It was an hour's ride on my bike. St. Mathew's Drug House was an impressive building, right in the heart of town. The dust and noise from the bus stand opposite were annoying. I introduced myself at the counter and asked to see the manager. In just a few moments, I was taken to his glass cabin.

"Welcome, Doctor." A kindly old man got up from his chair and extended his hand. "I've heard a lot about you. It is great work you are doing there! You see, I am married from Chittar. My father-in-law is your patient and he always speaks highly of you. You seem to have got his diabetes under control."

I sat in the heavily cushioned visitor's chair. The cabin was free from the dust and noise outside and I felt cool and comfortable under the breeze of the fan, sipping on the cold lemonade that was brought in for me. He must be a shrewd businessman with this over-friendly business behavior. But his warmth seemed to be genuine. Is this the guy fleecing our hospital with inflated drug bills?

I came down to business. "I've come to buy medicines for the hospital. But before that, I want to be clear about the pricing. It seems you are taking too much- especially considering that we are purchasing in bulk."

His face changed to one of utter seriousness. "In fact doctor, I can give you all medicines at twenty percent less than what we are charging now. But then we can't afford to pay commission to anyone."

I could not believe my ears. Mathai Sir was the senior-most member in the local committee, the headmaster of the Sunday School, and the representative of the local parish in the church assembly. How could he do this?

"He is a much-respected man locally in Chittar," I protested.

"I know, Doctor, I had even thought of refusing him. But I know that then he will just go to my competitor nearby, who might even agree to increase the bill up to thirty percent!"

I felt a rage within me. *Why was Mathai Sir taking advantage? Is it why the hospital had not prospered all these years?*

"I can tell you an even better way," he continued. "I can direct the medical representatives of various companies to your hospital, and you can place your orders directly with them. You will get an even lower price and you may receive lots of free samples that you can use to help your poor patients."

I felt his words were too good to be true. "But then will you not lose your business with us?"

"See doctor, I have a good flourishing business. I earn enough and more to keep myself fed. My children are grown up and are on their own. This is the least I can do, to help you with the work you are doing there. My only request is, please don't quit!"

Riding back home with the large cardboard box of medicines strapped to the back seat of my bike, I was feeling elated. Neither the fury of the sun nor the stifling cloud of smoke and dust had any effect on me. I tried to calculate how much Mathai Sir had been earning from this. Surely it would be more than thrice my monthly salary! And if the new system of directly purchasing from companies works out, it should be possible to save nearly seven thousand rupees every month! I will soon be able to upgrade our lab and other facilities.

Medical reps started arriving shortly. Most of them were seeing Chittar for the first time. "I have already purchased medicines for a month. I will need supplies only by next month," I told them.

"It's okay, doctor. You can give the order now. We will supply by next month, and you need to pay the bill only forty-five days after the supply."

They would leave lots of free samples. *Now I won't have to strain the hospital finances for giving help to poor patients. I can dole out these free medicines.*

Once the system became regular, they started bringing personal gifts also for us. We would accept those which were not too expensive. We thus acquired enough common utensils like plates, cups, flasks, and casseroles.

There would be some who would try to corrupt us with offers of money if I agree to inflated bills. I would usually politely decline but had to angrily show the door to a few of them who kept on persisting.

A surprising gift I once received other than from a medical rep. was from the footwear shop! He came with a large, multi-layered cake he had specially ordered from Pathanamthitta. "Doctor, since you arrived here, I am having record sales! Many are new customers. They say you have told them to buy chappals."

It was true that I had recommended many to use footwear having detected severe anemia in them. (Anemia is the decrease in the content of hemoglobin, the oxygen-carrying pigment in the blood. It gives the blood its bright red color, and its deficiency would make the patient pale, sometimes even causing breathlessness and palpitation. Examination of their stool sample would usually reveal hookworm infestation. Hookworms present in the soil, get into the body by penetrating through the skin of the soles. Wearing chappals would prevent this.) The quacks were loading them with iron-containing capsules, but they were not improving.

"I advise footwear for a reason," I told him. "I have not recommended specifically your shop to anyone."

"Mine is the only footwear shop in Chittar, Doctor. But till now, I haven't had any decent sales."

I accepted his gift with a request not to repeat.

11. Sub Inspector Sunny

Not all patients coming to the hospital were cooperative- Sometimes we got very unruly and troublesome ones. Most of these were alcoholics. The country-made arrack was their staple drink.

I certainly was not one to take any abuse lying down. I would react in equal if not greater measure. Sometimes I had to resort to physical methods. I was emboldened by the presence of the other regular patients. They would intervene to make sure that no harm comes to their doctor. Once I had to physically push out an unruly fellow right up to the road.

"Is this a doctor? Is this how a doctor would behave?" he shouted, addressing the crowd which had gathered.

"If you come to me as a patient, I will behave like a doctor. But if you come to me as a rowdy, I will also be a one," I retorted and walked back to the OP.

It was not only within the hospital, that drunkards were causing trouble. On their way back home from the liquor shops at night, many would be shouting out the filthiest of obscenities, though to no one in particular. I thought I should put an end to this. I didn't want Aju, who had just started talking, to be learning these words.

The first word that Aju spoke was "Ayyappo". He had learned it from the Sabarimala pilgrims trekking through the road, chanting "Swamiye! Ayyappo, Ayyappo! Swamiye." This chanting could be heard constantly even throughout the night during the peak season.

Once when my parents were visiting me with my brother and his family, Aju was on his usual chanting spree- "Ayyappo! Ayyappo!" walking around, balancing a book on his head in place of the irumudi kettu- the cloth bundle of traditional offerings, carried by the pilgrims.

My mother got very upset. "What is it with this boy? The first word he has learned is that of a Hindu God! Make him unlearn that, and teach him to chant 'Jesus! Jesus'!"

My brother burst out in a guffaw. "I will tell you an interesting story that happened a few months back," he began.

"I went to visit the Nilackal church and the Sabarimala temple with some of my friends. On the way, our jeep went off the road and turned over. Fortunately, none of us got hurt. At the church, the priest welcomed us and after hearing the story of the accident, he exclaimed- 'It is by the blessings and grace of St. Thomas that you escaped miraculously. You should stay for the service and take part in the communion, to give thanks to the saint.' I said sorry, we are in a hurry, we have to visit Sabarimala temple also before getting back home. The priest thought for a moment and pronounced- 'No wonder your jeep overturned!"

My father was amused, hearing this. "Don't interfere with Aju's natural learning process," he advised.

Anyhow, I didn't want the next word that Aju learned to be a vulgar one.

The next time a drunkard was mouthing obscenities, I went out and confronted him. He tried to argue, but I caught him by the scruff of the neck and threatened him so strongly, that he quietened down. Soon, the drunkards were subdued enough that all those creating scenes went quiet while passing through the stretch of road between the hospital and my quarters.

Some days later, there was a new guy shouting vulgarities on the road. When I confronted him, he started retaliating with lewd expletives. I lost my cool and gave him a hard blow on the face. He fell motionless. I panicked. Stooping down beside him, I checked his pulse. He was alive. I shook him hard but elicited no response. I fetched the BP apparatus from the hospital and checked his blood pressure. Everything seemed okay. *He must be malingering.*

I called aside the crowd of neighbors who had gathered, and whispered to them. "I think the guy is just acting. We will go back to our houses and watch what he does. If he doesn't get up, I'll have to inform the police." As we all watched through our windows, we could see him getting up after some time. He looked around and left quietly.

Another day, a well dressed drunken man who had come with his mother started creating a ruckus at the hospital. He kept on abusing the staff, not heeding his mother's weak protests. He was finally thrown out with the help of the other patients waiting, and the neighbors who had come in hearing the commotion. I decided to visit the police station with a written complaint.

The Sub Inspector (SI) in charge was a fair, handsome young man who had just joined in his new posting. He was very professional. After having heard me out, he accepted my complaint, read through it, and issued me a receipt. "Don't worry, Doctor. We will handle this," he assured me. I thanked him and rose to leave.

"Please sit for some time, Doctor. I would like to know you. How come you are working in this place? If you are not in a hurry, we will just visit my quarters in the adjacent building. I would also like you to meet my wife.

His wife was equally fair and beautiful. *What a handsome couple.* We sat talking for quite some time. His name was Sunny. He seemed glad to have finally met an educated person in Chittar. As for his education, he had amassed such a lot of degrees that would put a college professor to shame.

"How did you collect so many degrees?" I asked incredulously.

"It is a hobby with me, Doctor," he answered with a smile. "I like to be forever learning. After college, I joined for various degrees one after the other, in universities having postal courses."

His wife brought tea for us. It was delicious and flavored with cardamom. As I left, he came with me up to my bike. "There is just one regret I have, Doctor. We have been married for three years now, but we are yet to have a child. Our parents are bothering us with their anxiety."

"Why don't you come to the hospital one day? I would like to know the details as well as give you a preliminary examination."

"I wouldn't like to do that, Doctor. Being the SI here, I would like to keep my privacy. If I need a detailed check-up, I would prefer to go to Trivandrum. But I don't know when it will be possible."

"Come home for a visit with your wife one day. I would like to give you some tips which can boost your chances of conceiving."

Sunny came to the hospital the next day itself. "We have traced the person who created trouble for you. He is now at the station. It seems he is a teacher at the government school. He is fervently pleading for forgiveness. He is willing to apologize to any extent. If you pursue the complaint and this case is charged, he stands the risk of even losing his job."

What kind of teacher is this? Are all the teachers here like this? Just a few months back, I had to attend to a child who had been severely punished by a teacher in the same school, for not having completed his homework. There were red and blue bruises on his legs and back. His father had told me that he was going to complain to the headmaster. This teacher would beat only those boys who do not buy him liquor. Others would escape punishment by supplying him enough arrack to drink. *Once Aju grows up, where will I send him to school?*

"I would prefer not to see this guy again," I told Sunny. "If you can get him to give a written apology, I will withdraw my complaint. I just want to make sure that he will not trouble us again."

"Don't worry doctor, I will see to that. By the way, are you free tonight? I would like to come and visit you with my wife.

"Please come, but I am never totally free at any time. Just like you, I am always on duty. I will have to attend any call from the hospital in between, but we'll hope that there will be no calls this evening."

They arrived at six o'clock in a hired jeep. Sunny was very particular about taking anyone other than official persons in the police jeep, even his wife. "We are just about to prepare supper. Will you also join?" I asked.

"Sorry doctor, we'll make it some other time. Today's dinner has already been prepared and is ready at home."

His wife joined Jessy in the kitchen, and I sat talking with him on the front veranda. We sipped homemade pineapple wine, which he liked. It was a heady strong drink, and we both felt the effect. I gave him a detailed lecture on how best they can increase their chances of conceiving- when is the time during the monthly cycles that they should be having sex, how she should lie with her back raised over a pillow for some time after the act, how dipping his testicles in cold water and avoiding tight underclothes can increase the sperm count, and so on.

I gave him all the tips I could think of. "But you'll have to visit a gynecologist and get both of you thoroughly checked without much delay if nothing works."

I didn't notice that Aju had climbed up onto his lap. He stretched up and kissed Sunny on his cheek. I saw the SI's face turning red. He gave back the kiss holding him in a tight hug. "This is a new experience for me!" he exclaimed. "I've never been kissed by a child like this!"

Sunny became a regular visitor in the evenings. When I got a call from the hospital, he would wait at home playing with Aju, till I returned. Word went around that the new SI and the doctor are great friends. Troublemakers in the hospital and the drunkards around no longer created any problem for us.

A few months later, Sunny was exuberant when he came to visit us in the evening. "Doctor, my wife is pregnant!" he exclaimed, obviously very thrilled. He had brought chocolates for us. "We had been religiously following whatever advice you gave. I am so grateful."

After he left, I turned to Jessy. "I think, more than my instructions, it must have been Aju's influence that did the trick. Haven't you heard about couples who had been childless for years, conceiving soon after they adopt a child?"

My friendship with the SI proved beneficial on several other occasions- especially when we had the birth of another illegitimate child in the hospital.

12. Sally, Johnykutty, and Depressive Illnesses

It was a busy morning. I didn't immediately recognize the two men who came in. I glanced at the file. Johnykutty! He had changed a lot. He was much thinner and had dark circles around his eyes. "Doctor, you must help me! I am not able to sleep a wink. I don't feel like eating anything."

"Please give him some good advice Doctor," his father interrupted. "He won't even go to work. The jeep is lying almost idle. I know his real problem." He looked accusingly at his son. "He has not yet got that girl Sally out of his head. It seems she has cast a spell upon him like she must have done to many others."

"Don't be so hard on her," I told them. I explained how Sally had confessed to us about her pregnancy. "It was a moment's indiscretion." I then described to them how when Sally's father had come to pay the bill, he had described her situation, which was quite similar to Johnykutty's present state.

- 54 -

I could see Johnykutty perking up, on hearing about Sally.

"Yes," Johnykutty's father was reflective. "She really was very charming, well mannered and always helpful around the house. But there is no way we can accept someone else's child into our family."

"We will wait and see," I said. "I understand that she is now in Kasaragod. I had told them to come here one day, once they return. Meanwhile Johnykutty, you have to pull yourself together. Brooding all the time and not going to work will only make matters worse. I also want you to take some medicines."

I knew it would take some time for him to get back to normal. I had always been fascinated by the effect of psychiatric medicines and always stocked the essential ones. Many patients were relieved from years of distress by the introduction of these new medicines.

I remember a lady in particular who had come to me with the complaint that her daughter-in-law was trying to kill her with a slow poison mixed in her food. I knew the girl too. She was a regular visitor with her kids. Her husband was away, working in the army. She was under considerable strain, looking after the children and her in-laws.

I started the lady on a low dose antipsychotic drug. The next time she came to visit, she was very happy. "My daughter-in-law is still poisoning me, but the poison is not having any effect on me because of your medicines." I felt only a partial success, as she was still having her delusions. However, there was not much problem in the family thereafter.

I wrote down a prescription of some antidepressants for Johnykutty. "Hope your sleep and general mood will improve with this. See you in two weeks."

Soon after I had finished my morning OP, Lissy came in. "Wasn't that Sally's husband and father who had come earlier today? Did they say anything?"

Lissy was always very active in collecting and spreading gossip. "Why?"

I asked.

"Didn't you hear the news, Doctor? Sally and her parents have come back from Kasargod. They claim that the child died of a serious fever while they were there, and he has been buried there itself. But no one believes them. Everybody thinks that they must have murdered the child!"

My heart sank, and my mind went numb. Even I found it hard to believe that the child, an exceptionally healthy baby would suddenly succumb to a fever. But then, the faces of Sally and her father flashed through my mind. I certainly could not imagine them to be capable of murder!

Sally herself made her appearance with her father a few days later. She looked haggard and depressed, but even in this state, she radiated a serene beauty.

"Doctor, you have to do something. Sally is now worse than before. She refuses to take food. She doesn't even help her mother in the kitchen. She just lies all day brooding." Sally's father seemed desperate.

"I heard that the child has died?" I inquired. Both of them didn't answer. They just sat there with downcast eyes. *Guilt may be haunting them.*

"I recently had a patient with exactly the same symptoms," I said. "You know him. It is Johnykutty."

I saw Sally looking up, scanning my face for some information. "I thought they might eventually be ready for reconciliation, especially since the problem of the child has been taken care of," I added a bit sarcastically. Sally's face changed to one of hope and expectancy.

I prescribed for Sally the same medicines I had given to Johnykutty. "See me again in two weeks," I said and proceeded to the next patient. When the patient left, Sally and her father were again at the door.

"May we come in, Doctor? We want to tell you something."

I nodded for them to come in. Sally's father came and sat close to me.

Making sure that nobody could overhear him, he asked me in a hushed voice. "Doctor, do you suspect that we killed the child?" This time, I didn't answer. "Can you believe that we are capable of such an act? He is alive and well."

I looked at him with a puzzled expression.

"Sally was insisting on me to tell you the truth. Please do keep it absolutely confidential. My cousin in Kasargod had actually planned everything. She had contacted an orphanage there. They were willing to take him. We have signed and given documents giving up all our rights to the child. When we came back without the child, people started talking. We told everyone that he suddenly fell severely ill and died, but many think that we have done away with him."

I sat thinking, as the information sank in. "I want to share this with just three people," I said. "You should allow me. It is Johnykutty and his parents. I do have a faint hope of you reconciling, but anyone will be wary of people they suspect to be murderers. I will tell them to keep it a secret."

Lissy came in soon after they left. "Did they say anything about the child, Doctor?"

"Yes," I replied. "It seems he got a sudden acute illness that caused his death. I think it must have been pneumonia." She left, looking a bit skeptical.

Exactly on the day that I had asked Johnykutty to come for review, he turned up with his father. He looked much better. His father seemed relieved. "He is at least taking some food now," he reported."

"I am also sleeping better," Johnykutty added. "I have started working too!"

"We heard that Sally and family are back," his father said. "They say that the boy died of a fever. I think they have killed him!"

"No!" Johnykutty seemed much bolder now. "I am sure they won't do anything like that. Sally wouldn't even harm a fly!"

After extracting from them an assurance that they would keep it confidential, I related to them all that I had learned. "Please keep your promise not to divulge this to anyone."

"You have my word, Doctor. Moreover, if ever we decide someday to take back Sally, it is better to keep it that way. Let people think that the child is dead."

I noticed that he was moving towards the idea of accepting Sally back into their house. And I knew Johnykutty was only too eager! I hoped the day would not be too far away.

Sunny made an unexpected visit a few days later.

"My visit is actually official, Doctor." I could see the change of behavior in him when on official duty. "Many have reported to me about the possible infanticide of a child born here to a lady named Sally. I heard it was an illegitimate child whom they took to Kasaragod and killed it there. Nobody has given me a formal complaint yet, but it is sure to come. I thought I would make a preliminary inquiry."

I was in a fix. I will have to break my word if I am to tell him everything, but informing him of the facts will only be in the best interests of both the families.

I gave him the actual facts. "But if it is known that the child is still alive, it might complicate things for them. I believe they are on the path of reconciliation."

"Don't worry," Sunny assured me. "I can confirm their story by inquiries with our station in Kasaragod. If it is confirmed that there has been no homicide, I can tell any litigant that we have enquired and found that the child had a natural death."

13. The Hardy Tribes

The hospital had acquired a reputation far and wide that even tribals living deep inside the forest started arriving when they felt their illness to be too serious to be managed by their tribal doctor. I never ceased to be amazed by the rugged hardiness of those folks.

A middle-aged man once came asking for a tetanus injection. He had fallen off a tree, and a sharp rock had cut a deep, long laceration on his leg.

"I have managed the injury, doctor. I just need the injection," he said displaying the wound. It had been neatly stapled with ten safety pins. "I did it myself," he proclaimed proudly.

I saw that it was closed with a good approximation of the edges. "But this should have been cleaned and sterilized before suturing," I lectured him. "The safety pins may be contaminated."

"I cleaned the wound with boiled water and each safety pin was held over the fire before inserting it," he replied.

I gave the tetanus shot and persuaded him to take a course of antibiotics, leaving the sutured wound as such.

Once I was called to the hospital late in the night. A woman in labor had been brought from her hut in the forest, carried on a bed by four men through eight kilometers of the jungle path. She had been in labor for more than sixteen hours and was badly fatigued.

The midwife had suggested that she be taken to the hospital fast. I could manage her with intravenous fluids to relieve her exhaustion and a vacuum-assisted delivery.

The most remarkable encounter I've had with a tribal patient was on an early summer morning when he was carried in, gored by a wild boar on the back of the thigh and buttock. Blood was flowing freely from the gaping wound.

Quickly washing and mopping up the area, I was relieved to find the major artery was intact, but many of its branches were torn and bleeding. I asked for artery forceps and clamped the bleeding points one by one till we had exhausted all the sterilized ones we had in stock. There were still many more areas where blood was oozing. Swiftly, I tied up the vessels already clamped, so that we could take out some of them, and clamp them to other sites still bleeding.

Finally, I had the bleeding controlled. The injury could now be clearly seen. The large thick muscle on the buttock was torn across but for a shred at the outer border. The stout nerve supplying nerves to virtually the whole leg was exposed all the way into the thigh - as I had never seen even in the anatomy dissection hall of medical school.

Throughout this, the young man lay still. He reeked strongly of alcohol. I called in his elder brother.

"I have done all that is possible here. The bleeding is controlled, but there is a lot of damage to the muscles and other tissues. You have to take him to Pathanamthitta and get it repaired by an experienced surgeon."

I firmly stood my ground when he protested, asking me to handle him myself. I felt a tug on my shirt. The injured man pulled me towards him. "Please doctor, don't send me away. We can't afford to go to town. We won't be able to survive there. I will lie absolutely still, for you to stitch it."

I had to agree. I worked on it for more than two hours, suturing the tissues layer by layer. True to his word, he lay absolutely still, answering my queries. His name was Muthuswamy. He lived in a tree house in the forest with his wife and daughter. The only neighbors were his brother and family on another tree. They earned their livelihood by gathering honey, incense, and cardamom from the forest. He would hunt wild boars for their meat with crude spears. It was while thus hunting, he was gored from behind by its mate.

Finally closing the skin, I wondered if I had overstretched my domain. I found a plank of wood which I strapped down from his chest to below the thigh so that he wouldn't be able to bend his hip and stretch the muscles held together with the sutures.

He was admitted for ten days. Dressings were done daily. High dose antibiotics were pumped in. The injury showed signs of healing, and the sutures were removed. "You will be able to go home tomorrow", I informed him during the evening rounds. "But you will have to stay in bed for another two weeks."

He asked me to give an estimate of his total bill. I did a rough calculation and told him that the bill would come to around five hundred rupees. *I can reduce some amount for him tomorrow.*

Early the next morning, Chackochan came to inform that the patient was not to be seen in the ward. "He seems to have absconded without paying the bill."

"The ungrateful wretch!" I cursed under my breath, thinking of all the trouble we had taken for his treatment.

A couple of months later, while I was getting ready to leave for duty, I had a visitor. I recognized him immediately as Muthuswami. Before I could say anything, he placed a large bundle at my doorstep.

"I am so sorry I left that day without telling you. There was no way I could pay the bill. I hope this will cover it," he said, opening the sack. There were twelve bottles of honey, a big paper bag full of cardamom, and a cute little bamboo basket filled with incense.

"But the value of all this must be higher than your bill amount," I protested.

"That is only when you go to purchase it from a shop, Doctor. We don't even get half that amount." He thanked me profusely, apologizing again for having absconded that day. "My leg is perfectly alright now. I could even hunt down another wild boar."

I wondered how I would pay the hospital. That had to be done in cash. I decided to settle the bill from my pocket, and take his offering for myself. There was such a lot of stuff, so the next time my parents came to visit, I sent with them enough cardamom, honey, and incense to be distributed to all our relatives and friends. I made the rest into small packets and distributed them to all the staff.

Lissy came into my room. "Thank you so much for the gift, Doctor. The cardamom is of excellent quality. You won't get such good ones in any of the shops."

"You should thank Muthuswamy," I said. She lingered on. I knew she had some gossip to share. "Yes Lissy, what is the latest?"

"Doctor, did you know that Sally and Johnykutty are again together?"

"Really?" I exclaimed. "Are you sure?" Happiness engulfed me. It had been some time since I've seen either of them. I had given anti-depressants to both of them for one month asking for a review afterward. Cleverly, I had given the same appointment date hoping something to work out in a chance encounter, but neither had turned up.

"I got the information from Sally's neighbors," Lissy continued, looking a bit offended that I was skeptical about the news from her. "They had gone to the police station to register a complaint on the suspicion that the child was killed while in Kasargod. S.I. Sir promised them that he would conduct a thorough investigation and a week later, he confirmed that the child had died of pneumonia in the Government Hospital there. After that, these people who had been shunning Sally's family became friendlier to them and were in fact instrumental in her reunion with Johnykutty."

14. At last, A Decent Lab

I was puzzled by the large number of diabetic patients. This was supposed to be a disease of the affluent! Each day I was detecting at least one new case of diabetes. Ideally, the patient's blood should be tested for sugar level, to make the diagnosis. Since we didn't have the facility, we had to go by the urine.

It was the age-old Benedict test. You had to take five milliliters of the blue reagent in a test tube, add ten drops of urine and boil it. If the urine contained sugar, the color would change according to its level, to green, yellow, or orange, and it will be a brick red for the highest level. Lissy would send in the written reports along with the patient's files, but when it was brick red, she would come in to display the test tube, holding it aloft as if she had won a trophy.

There were also the already diagnosed patients, usually managed by the local quacks with the anti-diabetic tablets that were available then. They doled out these tablets in increasingly heavy doses, with no advice about diet or exercises. The only dietary advice given was to reduce sugar intake. Most of these patients were poorly controlled in spite of receiving the highest dose of drugs.

If any such patient came to the OP it would take a hell of a lot of time to explain how to watch the calorie intake, reduce carbohydrates, increase veggies, and explain the importance of exercise. I thought tapioca was a major culprit and many of them were having it three times a day! We could slowly control the disease in those who came for regular follow up. Still, there were many without proper control.

We have to have insulin. The reason I did not pursue it much earlier was that only very few of our patients had a refrigerator at home, and insulin had to be stored in one.

Anyway, we started stocking insulin and started some of the uncontrolled patients on it, with dramatically good results. Many kept their insulin at the nearest house having a fridge and would go there morning and evening for their jabs. Some of them developed the innovative method of keeping it wrapped in plastic and buried in fine sand in an earthen pot, frequently sprinkled with water. It seemed to work very well and I began recommending it to all who reported not having a fridge.

One day, a diabetic patient was brought in a very bad state. He was stuporous and breathing heavily. I looked him over and found his tongue was parched and dry- obviously severely dehydrated. His breath had the smell of over-ripe bananas that had begun to rot- a sure sign of ketoacidosis, a serious complication of uncontrolled diabetes when acetone levels also go high, and get excreted in the breath and urine.

His life was in danger. I put in a catheter to collect some urine which revealed after the test to be high in sugar and acetone. There was no doubt about the diagnosis now. We started him on intravenous fluids, antibiotics and hourly insulin. I explained the condition to the relatives and asked them to take him to town. As usual, they refused and insisted that he be treated here.

Having warned them of the risks including the possibility of death, I proceeded with the treatment relying solely on the urine test hourly, for calculating the dose of insulin shots. Fortunately, he started responding after a few hours and could be discharged in two days. *At any cost, I have to buy a calorimeter and be able to check blood sugar. We can afford one now.*

I set off early morning to Trivandrum on my bike. It was after a gap of ten months that I was visiting the city, which had been my home for seven years- initially as a medical student, then as a house surgeon, and later as a junior doctor in a private hospital. I felt a sense of homecoming.

I fought off a compelling desire to make a visit to the Medical College just eight kilometers away. Many of my friends would be there. Some were doing postgraduate courses in various specialties. A good number will still be undergraduates, not yet having cleared the final exam. Anyway, I could not afford time for that. I had to reach back before evening- otherwise, Jessy will have trouble looking after Aju while attending to calls from the hospital.

The medical equipment store was in the heart of the city. I chose a reasonably good model of a photo-calorimeter costing just above rupees four thousand. I had it packed and billed, then took out the cheque-book and started writing down the amount.

The proprietor of the shop stopped me, holding my hand. "No Doctor, sorry I can't accept a cheque from you. You have to pay in cash."

"But I don't have that kind of cash on me! This bank account belongs to the hospital."

"You must understand, Doctor. I don't know you. We are meeting for the first time, and you say you are coming from a place that I've never even heard of. What if the cheque bounces?"

I knew his argument was valid. Having come with great hopes, going back without the instrument would be depressing. How can I convince him? I did have a few relatives in Trivandrum, but they lived in the outskirts. Going just to one place would make the rest of them my enemies for life. It would also mean I would take up too much time.

Suddenly, I had a thought. Surely, he will know the professors in Medical College. I had been a bad student but was an obedient and sincere house surgeon. They will endorse me.

"See, I studied here in Trivandrum Medical College. Are there any professors you know there, from whom you can check about me?"

"Of course! We are their regular suppliers. But all the doctors there will be busy now in the wards or in the OP." He paused, thinking. It seemed like he was beginning to feel some pity for me. "There's the Principal. He will be in the office now. I know him very well. Shall I call him? Will he know you?"

My heart skipped a beat. *He knows me only too well!* I had been active in student politics and he had been a strong disapprover- especially of my leftist leanings. I've even had a few altercations with him in his office. But I hoped that he had no personal animosity towards me. "Okay," I said feebly.

"Of course I know him! What's that guy doing there?" I could hear clearly the Principal's voice at the other end. The shop owner explained to him the circumstances. The voice at the other end was now softer and inaudible.

"He wants to speak to you." The owner of the store handed me the phone.

"So you have passed the course and left college? That's why I am not troubled by you nowadays! Now, where is this place you say you are working?"

I explained to him about the hospital in Chittar and how I had gone to work in such a remote place of my own will.

"Good, but be sure to work hard in your studies and get entry into a post-graduate course. From next year, we are having entrance exams for the PG courses."

I tried the same trick that had succeeded with my father. I explained how being a specialist will be of no use in such a place.

"It's your decision. But I am warning you. Ultimately, you will have to look after yourself and your family on your own. There is no future for a just-MBBS doctor. The future belongs to the specialist. Okay, now give the phone to Mr. Mathew."

They spoke for a few minutes, and when they hung up, Mathew was smiling. "It seems you were a troublesome student there, Doctor. But obviously, he likes you and trusts you. Now give me that cheque."

Riding towards the city center with the precious instrument tied up firmly on my back seat, I passed the studio where I had taken a post-wedding black and white photo with Jessy, while we were house surgeons there. It had come out so good. Both of us looked great in it. I felt like going in to thank the artist who touched it up. I shrugged off the childish thought. It seems I have now even started thinking like a crude villager!

I was starting to feel hungry. I stepped into Azad hotel and ordered chicken biryani. It had been quite some time since I've had one.

The ride back was uneventful. I made it slowly, praying no harm had been caused to the calorimeter by the bumps and potholes. The cool and dust-free breeze soon as I crossed the 'Boundary' could not be missed.

Lissy was handling a calorimeter for the first time. She had seen one at the lab where she studied, but the students were not allowed to touch it. We went in detail through the user manual. I had bought kits for testing glucose, renal function, cholesterol, and bilirubin.

We decided on starting with the blood sugar kit first. I volunteered to be the guinea pig.

When Lissy came in with my result, it showed a blood sugar level of only thirty-eight! I should be in a coma with such a low level!

"Do you have some left over sample? We will try again, and I will watch you do it."

Lissy was visibly nervous and started sucking in the small quantity of serum, using the micropipette. "Wait!" I shouted and snatched the pipette from her. I saw it was wet. Water droplets were clearly visible in the tube. "This water will dilute my sample. No wonder you got me such a low result."

Even after making sure that the pipette was dry and doing the test together, we came up with a reading of seventy-two. Though better, it was still not logical, especially since I had just had my breakfast.

"We will wait to be confident about this before using it on patients" I declared and left the lab. I felt like the proverbial monkey with a coconut that could not be dehusked. All through that day, my thoughts were on the calorimeter. *Did I get defective equipment?* Unlikely, since it was from a reputed company. I finally made up my mind and called Lissy in.

"Sister Moncy is getting married and will be leaving shortly. I want you to replace her and work as a nursing assistant. Meanwhile, I will try to get someone experienced in biochemistry as the new lab technician."

Lissy looked crestfallen. "Please give me one or two weeks, Doctor. I will sort things out."

Four days later, she walked in with her husband, who had just landed from Kuwait. He was an experienced and well-qualified lab technician working in a major hospital there. "I took emergency leave, Doctor. Lissy here wanted me to come immediately and train her to use the calorimeter you had purchased."

The following week, he gave intensive training to his wife and by the time he left, Lissy was an expert. People from many kilometers around started pouring in, ours being the only hospital with a lab that could do biochemical tests. The morning rush in the OP became almost unmanageable.

15. Water, Diarrhea, and Avarachen

Water was a problem during the summer. The level of water in the well had gone down, and pumping became possible only once a day. If pumping was not stopped before the water level got too low, air would get into the pump. The first time we faced this problem, there was fortunately, a plumber among the patients waiting. He showed us how to open the valve attached to the motor and pour in water to expel the air so that the pump would work again.

As the summer progressed, the water level got too low and Chackochen would have to fetch water from the house just opposite to the hospital. Pappychayan was the head of the family of nine, living in the small house, with his sons and their wives and kids. He was also an active member in the church, but never held any official post. Their income was from trading rubber sheets that they bought from the local small growers and selling them to the agents. They also traded in pepper and other spices.

Being a mild diabetic and BP patient, he used to come for regular check-ups. His family members also came occasionally with minor illnesses. They never ever asked for any concession in the bill. But when it came to helping the hospital for anything, they would do it as if it was their own institution.

Summer months were also the time when lots of patients got admitted with vomiting and diarrhea. Frequently using the toilets, they would quickly deplete the water. I felt bad seeing the aged Chackochan fetching water frequently from Pappychayan's well. He would make numerous trips with a large aluminum pot balanced on his head and carrying a large plastic bucket in one hand. He did the job without complaint. My suggestion that he be paid an extra allowance for this work was unanimously turned down- 'That is part of his work.'

The patients with diarrhea would need replacement for the fluid lost. Sometimes, it would become necessary to give them intravenous fluids. But if it was not that serious and there was not much vomiting, we advised them to take plenty of oral fluids.

Kanji water- the water drained after cooking rice- with added salt was the most preferred. I would ask the patients to get this from Pappychayan's house. They always kept kanji water ready for any patients who might need it. Pappychayan once came to ask me how much salt should be ideally added. I could only marvel at his attitude. He did not do it as a help, but as if it was his duty.

Patients with severe diarrhea will usually survive if they are kept hydrated enough. Only those very ill with infection would need the addition of antibiotics. Deaths due to diarrhea and dehydration were not uncommon in the area. Luckily, we didn't have a single diarrheal death at the hospital throughout our period there, though once we came pretty close.

It was a young five-year-old boy. He had been having lots of watery stools for the past three days, while also running a high fever. He was taken to Avarachan for treatment. Avarachan was not exactly a quack. He was a qualified homeopathic doctor- although he never ever practiced homeopathy. His pharmacy was never stocked with even a single homeopathic drug, but he had many of the modern drugs including powerful antibiotics always stocked and used lavishly.

This boy was also put on Lomotil,, antibiotics and paracetamol but he became worse. He was also not passing urine. His parents took him again to Avarachan.

"Not passing urine?" he asked. "We will rectify that with this injection." Few minutes after the injection, the boy passed urine. But before they had time to rejoice, he collapsed and that's how he was brought here.

The boy was unconscious. I felt the skin over his stomach. When pinched, it stayed up just like that- wrinkled up like a piece of cloth. His tongue was dry as the desert. Checking with my stethoscope, I could hear a faint, rapid heartbeat. He was still alive.

We have to quickly get lots of fluid into him! But there was no way we could put in an IV needle. All his veins had collapsed. I tried to get into a vein blindly through multiple pricks with a tiny butterfly needle, but nowhere could I strike blood. *There is no other way but to do a cut-down.*

I had never done a cut-down before, but I have seen it being done a couple of times. I congratulated myself on my foresight to have directed my staff to always have a cut-down set ready for use.

Without bothering about any anesthesia, I took the scalpel to cut across through the skin over the shin, just above the ankle. Dissecting down through the tissues, my heart gave a leap as I saw the vein sneaking upwards over the bone and a thin layer of muscle. The rest of the procedure was easy. Holding up the vein with a pair of forceps, I put a tie, then made a small nick just above it, and passed in a cannula.

"Now quick! Connect the drip to this," I shouted to the sister as I fixed in the cannula and sutured up the wound. "Let it go at full speed!"

The boy survived, and the hospital thrived.

It turned out that the injection given by Avarachan was Lasix- a drug used in kidney diseases for fluid overload. Here, the young boy collapsed because it had pushed out the last reservoir of fluid left in his body.

The incident caused a drop in Avarachan's patients and an increase in ours. Many demanded that a case be brought up and get him arrested for quackery. I dissuaded them. If Avarachen was to close down, what about the 30-40 patients coming to see him every day? If all of them start coming to us, we certainly won't be able to manage the crowd.

I had at times felt envious of him. I knew he was earning many times more than we combined. He was the only person in the whole area who owned a private car. All others rich enough to buy a four-wheeler opted for a taxi- handy for their personal use, as well as earning them an income.

I decided it was unworthy to view him as an adversary. One day, I visited him at his clinic-cum-home just a few dozen meters away from my quarters. He welcomed me gracefully. We talked about the boy in a friendly way. I found him a bit too proud to be taking my advice, but I educated him on the importance of fluids to prevent dehydration in a patient with diarrhea. He realized his mistake.

A few months later, he came rushing to my OP. His father was having convulsions. I followed him briskly to his house. His father was having violent fits and was kept pressed down on the bed by several people. Assisted by Avarachen, I gave an IV injection of Calmpose, which he was having in his own pharmacy. The seizures subsided.

Avarachan's father has never been my patient, so I quickly got his medical history. He was a diabetic and had suffered a stroke several years back. He was on the blood-thinning drug Aspirin and Daonil, a powerful anti-diabetic. Could the blood thinners have caused a bleed in his brain? We have to take him to hospital, I declared. Avarachen agreed, though a bit reluctantly.

"How long has it been since his blood sugar has been last checked?" I asked.

"It must be a few years now," Avarachen replied. The last time must be when he was admitted in hospital with the stroke."

I asked Lissy for an emergency blood sugar test to be done. Not waiting for the result, I started a glucose infusion. The blood sugar report came in as thirty-two. It was way too low than the minimum level required. He was already recovering with the glucose drip.

"We have to reduce his drugs. Please see that he gets his blood sugar also checked at regular intervals," I advised Avarachen.

16. Broken Bones and Hearts

We were often getting cases of falls with fractures. The uncomplicated ones, I was managing there. A splint or slab was applied while pulling on the limb so that the pieces of bone fall into place . The patients were asked to come within three days with an X-ray, to see if the bones are well aligned. About ten percent didn't come back and of the rest, ninety percent returned without the X-ray. 'We can't afford to go to Pathanamthitta and take the X-ray, Doctor.'

Hoping that things will work out fine, I would proceed to blindly put on the plaster cast, strapping bandage cloth around the fractured area in layers, sprinkling Plaster of Paris powder and water in between the layers. After waiting till it became hard and stiff, they were sent home to report back after 6 weeks. On returning, the hard cast had to be laboriously cut open with a crude handheld saw.

Most of the fractures would come straight and nicely united, but occasionally you had these cases of malunion when the bones would have united at an angle, causing the arm or leg to be slightly bent, which the patients accepted as their fate. However, there had not been a single case of non-union- where the bones failed to unite. I gave credit to the ruggedness of villagers.

I knew I had to give up fantasies about acquiring an X-ray machine. It would cost a bomb, and maintaining it and having a full-time technician was obviously not viable. But certainly, I should get an ECG machine!

We had cases of severe chest pain coming almost daily. Often, it was due to acid regurgitation from the stomach. For many, chillies were the most favored ingredient in any dish. It would closely mimic a heart attack. There were those coming with a psychologically induced panic pain, more often among young women.

There was also the possibility of a real heart attack! Diagnosing each condition with just a clinical examination was really tricky.

Enquiries sent out by mail narrowed down the choice to the BPL office in Kochi, who offered to supply a basic model for rupees thirteen thousand. We might be able to save enough within two or three months, but I was not ready to wait. I wrote to Thirumeni asking for a loan of ten thousand rupees. He agreed.

It was another long trip on my bike to Kochi, the industrial capital of Kerala. This time, I made sure to carry a demand draft for payment.

The city was bustling with activity. Everyone, including the mosquitoes, seemed to be hard at work. I suddenly realized I had never seen one of these pesky insects in Chittar. The traffic was unbearable. *If you value your life, it is better to give ample berth to the buses and lorries wanting to overtake you. I like the quieter ambience of Trivandrum city more.*

The showroom manager was amused to see a doctor who had come riding hundred and fifty kilometres on his bike, from a part of land he had not heard of till then. He took pains to explain the working of the machine in great detail- including basic troubleshooting techniques. "We do have onsite servicing, but you might have to bring the machine at least to the nearest town in case of trouble," he warned.

The ECG machine turned out to be really handy. I noticed curiously that the proportion of patients presenting to the hospital with chest pain increased significantly ever since we acquired the machine. Several patients who were having serious risk factors for heart disease had their ECG taken for the first time. We were able to pick up many heart diseases at a much earlier stage. We would put them on blood-thinning medications, and impose tighter control over blood sugars, cholesterol and blood pressure. These measures would have added many more years to their lives.

Severe acute cases also began reporting frequently from very far off places. Pilgrims from Sabarimala were brought in sometimes. The strenuous trek up the Sabarimala hill was the cause of many pilgrims developing a cardiac pain during the climb. Our centre was the nearest where an ECG was available, even though it was an eighty-kilometre ride through forest roads. Some were already dead on arrival. Others with significant changes in the ECG were rushed to Pathanamthitta, after giving some loading drugs as first aid.

With the locals, referring them to another centre was easier said than done. "Just having an ECG machine doesn't make this a cardiac centre!" I used to plead. "Please take the patient to a hospital with better facilities!"

Many remained adamant, and I would have to manage them there. Most of them somehow survived. They and their relatives would shower us with gratitude. A few died. The deaths were accepted as inevitable.

The tracing paper for the ECG machine ran out in just two months. I needed immediate replacement.

"My son is now in Trivandrum and is coming home for the weekend.

I will ask him to bring some," Mathai Sir volunteered. I gratefully accepted the offer. A few days later, he came with three rolls of the tracing paper and a voucher on which he had written- ECG paper + travelling expenses- Rs. 550/-.

"But this will last for just a month," I exclaimed as I paid him.

"Don't worry, doctor. My son will be coming at least once every month."

I decided to send Chackochan the next time. He was a bit reluctant at first, as he had never traveled anywhere that far. I gave him detailed instructions and handed him a thousand rupees. "Buy as many as you get from this after your travelling expenses," I told him. He came back with a big bundle, along with a proper bill. There were enough rolls to last for much more than a year.

One Saturday night, I was playing with my son after dinner when Chackochan came running. "Doctor, come quickly! It is Krishnadas! He is having severe chest pain and is gasping for breath!"

Krishnadas was a local VIP. One of the richest men around, he had several businesses. Prominent among these was what was known as a 'blade company'. The 'blade' reference was derived from Shakespeare's Shylock.

He would give loans to the local merchants- mostly the fishmongers. The terms of service were that for every ninety rupees given out early morning before they go to Pathanamthitta to buy fish from the wholesale market, they will have to pay back a hundred rupees by night. I had done a mental calculation of the effective interest rate in this deal. It would come to about four thousand percent! And considering that the loan is given for only for twelve hours, the real interest rate would actually be double!

Krishnadas also virtually owned the market. The market was a large, open compound which would come to life two days every week. Wednesdays and Saturdays were the market days in Chittar. The hospital also used to have a higher turnover on those days. The panchayat would rent out the market place on a yearly basis to the highest bidder and he will have the right to the place for the whole year. Anyone who comes to the market to sell his products or other wares will have to pay rent as demanded, for the space allotted to him that day. Krishnadas had a goonda gang on his payroll to maintain his business and collect his dues.

When I reached the hospital, Krishnadas was screaming and writhing in the bed, forcefully clutching his chest. *Not very convincing for a heart attack.* Those in real pain would not be usually screaming like this. He had been one of the earliest people who had come for an ECG examination earlier. Though being a heavy alcoholic, diabetic and blood pressure patient, his ECG had been perfectly normal. Urging him to be quiet, I examined him. "I will take his ECG myself," I said and asked everyone to leave the room.

"You will now have to lie still, otherwise the device won't give a proper tracing," I told him and started to connect the wires on to his body. Once everyone left the room, Krishnadas was quiet. "This ECG looks perfectly normal- just like the one we took earlier," I told him when I was done. "I don't think there is any problem with your heart"

"Doctor, please don't tell the others what you just told me," Krishnadas told me in a soft, conspiratorial tone. "I want to be admitted for a few days. My son was creating trouble at home. I caught him drinking and scolded him, but he had the audacity to shout back at me, asking me if I can drink, why can't he!"

"Okay," I agreed. "But I can't just tell them you are having a heart attack. I will say you need observation for one or two days." I called the sister and asked her to give him a shot of Vitamin B complex injection and a mild sedative tablet. His family was very impressed that he was so much better within minutes of just one injection.

I felt pity for this supposedly powerful man, having to feign a heart attack and get admitted to the hospital to avoid a confrontation with his son. I thought of Paappichayan in the opposite house. How respectful and obedient his sons were to him. *That's the power of moral authority!*

17. Success and Failure

One of my greatest failures apart from the still-birth of Molly's baby, was a patient who had come at around two o'clock on a summer morning.

Awakened from a deep slumber, I strode to the hospital still half asleep. I did a quick examination of the patient who was complaining of an excruciating headache. Not finding any abnormality, I made a diagnosis of migraine. I prescribed some powerful painkillers and went back home to continue my sleep

At just about five, I was again called for the same case. He seems to have not received much relief from the pain and just a few moments back, he passed out. I quickly ran up the steps to the ward. I could not feel any pulse. He had no heartbeat either. He was dead!

It must have been an internal bleed in the brain which caused a sudden death like this. Maybe an aneurysm- a ballooning of the artery in the brain, which ruptured. I had just jumped to my diagnosis of a migraine.

I drew some consolation from the fact that he lost his life within three hours of coming here. Even if I had diagnosed serious brain injury and referred him immediately, it would have taken them at least four hours to reach a center with a facility for a CT scan.

*****

Successes also came unexpectedly. Selvan was a middle-aged plantation worker who was brought unconscious having collapsed suddenly during work. He had given no warning, except for complaining of a headache on waking up in the morning.

I was pretty much sure that this was a case of a bleed in the brain, and asked them to take him immediately to a major center in Trivandrum or Kochi. The relatives were reluctant and wanted him to be treated here. I was not going to relent on this one. I persisted, citing the lack of facilities here. But then his father came up to me.

"Doctor, if you admit him and treat him here, we will accept whatever be the outcome. But if you refuse, we are going to just take him back home. We certainly are not capable of taking him to any high-tech center."

I had worked with a senior neurologist in a private hospital in Trivandrum. He used to say- "There is nothing much we can do in case of a major stroke. What we can do is try to maintain the life of the patient, and give time for the brain to heal itself."

I decided to follow his advice. I put a tube through the nostril into the stomach so as to feed him and another tube to drain out urine. Some drugs to reduce the brain swelling and oxygen to increase its levels in the blood and better availability to the brain were all that could be done. After two weeks, his condition was the same. There was no sign of life except for his breathing, a pulse, and a heartbeat. I called his father into my room.

"Sorry," I said, "but there seems to be no sign of improvement. I don't see any point in keeping him here further. I think you better take him home."

"I understand, Doctor. I will make arrangements for a jeep to come tomorrow."

Early the next day, while I was getting ready for work, I heard a loud knock on my door. I could make out it was not Chackochan.

I opened the door to see Selvan's father and prepared myself for the worst.

"Doctor!" he spoke excitedly. "My son has opened his eyes! He was looking at me."

Selvan's discharge was cancelled. He improved bit by bit, and started making some incomprehensible sounds as if wanting to say something. Movements in the limbs slowly appeared. I advised some physiotherapy exercises which they followed diligently. When he was discharged after another two weeks, he walked out of the hospital, though with support.

*****

Promptly referring a case on time could get you much greater credit at times.

Preethi was a recently detected case of pregnancy. She had come for a regular antenatal check-up just two weeks back. One day, while I was busy in the OP, she was rushed in with severe pain in the lower abdomen. She complained of dizziness and while I was examining her, she passed out. I had to quickly get hold of her to prevent her from falling. I laid her on the floor. She was sweating profusely.

Kneeling down beside her, I felt for her pulse. It was extremely feeble.

Intravenous fluids were pumped in with her lying on the floor itself. After some time she regained consciousness. Feeling her abdomen, I found she was having pain on touch in the lower part. I was sure that it was a case of tubal pregnancy that had ruptured. *Her life is in danger!* I called in her father who seemed relieved that she looked better.

"You don't have any time to wait," I told him. "Take her straight to Thiruvalla as soon as possible. She needs immediate surgery." I had to impress upon him the urgency of the situation. "She might need blood. Take a few people along who will be willing to donate. She is O positive." A few young people who had brought their parents for a consultation immediately volunteered, and got into the jeep along with them.

A fortnight later, Preethi and her father came to see me with a large packet of exotic chocolates. "You saved my daughter's life, Doctor!" He explained how initially he had ignored my advice and took her to a hospital in Pathanamthitta. They were told that such a serious case can't be handled there, and was directed again to Thiruvalla. By the time they got there, she had again become unconscious.

The casualty doctor rushed her to the operation theatre after going through my letter of reference. Eight bottles of blood had to be transfused during and after the surgery. Everything went well thereafter, and here she was, beaming with gratitude.

I was grateful for the chocolates. Just the day before, Aju had asked for one. He had got the taste during a trip to Tiruvalla. I had tried all the shops in Chittar, but none of them had chocolate- only the hard, round sugar candy. I did not buy them fearing he might choke on it. I had felt bad that I was not able to satisfy his simple wish. Even after distributing to all the staff, there were enough chocolates for him to last several weeks.

Preethi's father became a great fan. He narrated how his daughter was saved by the doctor in the Mission Hospital, to everyone he met. Many patients coming to the hospital would appreciate me, having heard the story from him. I thought of the poor gynecologist who had labored under severe stress to perform the surgery on the collapsed patient. But for Preethi and her family, I was the hero.

18. More Friends

We had an unexpected visitor. He arrived riding a Bullet. It was a motorcycle that had always fascinated me. "Hi, Doctor!" He greeted me cheerily. "I just came to meet you, and get acquainted. I am an assistant manager in Chittar estate."

Chittar estate was the sprawling rubber plantation spread over a large part of Chittar. It was several hundred acres, spreading over to the border areas of the panchayat.

"Daniel George," he introduced himself. We sat talking. Though almost my age, he was a bachelor and lived a lonely life in the estate bungalow. He had an old butler and a large black Labrador for company. With his clean-shaven face and boyish look, I found it difficult to believe that we were of the same age. Our conversation was in English. He was not a Malayali, though he could converse in the language. His home was near Ooty, the famed hill station in Tamilnadu. It was after a long time that I had talked to anyone in English.

DG, as we came to call him later, noticed my violin case leaned up against the wall. "Do you play the violin? Can I hear you play?"

"Not now," I declined. "It's been a long time. It's not even kept tuned."

"Okay, but do get it tuned and ready soon. I have a guitar which I sometimes strum alone, humming a tune. We can try to combine. Plan to come to my place someday."

I was excited. It's been a long time since I've done anything like that. Aju seemed attracted to him and was sitting on his lap, fiddling with his bunch of keys.

We went to his bungalow in the estate on a Sunday evening. I had taken my violin properly tuned. We played several songs together- me on the violin and he strumming along on his guitar, his Labrador joining in for the vocals.

DG became a regular visitor. Aju would love his visits, waiting eagerly to play with him, both of them squatting on the floor.

"Can you come to Pathanamthitta with me on Sundays?" DG asked, looking up from the floor. "We have a choir there and we are planning for a concert. We want to sing Handel's Messiah. If you come, we can really boost up the bass."

I was thrilled, but hesitated. "Jessy will have to attend to all the calls from the hospital if I am away. It will be difficult for her."

"Go!" Jessy urged. "It will only be two or three hours. I will manage." She knew how badly I wanted to join them. Music was one area where we never connected- she had been born tone-deaf.

We traveled every Sunday to Pathanamthitta on his Bullet. It was a wonderful gang, but mostly all were amateurs. They liked my deep bass.

On the day of the concert, the hall was packed. I was not pleased with our rendering, but was pleasantly surprised by the loud applause after the Hallelujah chorus. The experts present came to us after the concert and reported their disappointment. I realized that all the choir members had brought friends and relatives as cheerleaders. "Anyway, Hallelujah Chorus has been sung in Pathanamthitta for the first time," DG comforted me.

One day he informed us that their company was planning to appoint a qualified doctor in their estate." Will you be interested? The hospital has only bare facilities but you will get a decent salary!"

It didn't sound attractive to me. I will have to abandon this hospital we have built up and work in a place without a lab or inpatient facilities. There won't be much scope for any meaningful treatments. The work will be mostly administrative in nature. Moreover, they had vacancies for only one medical officer.

Around three months later, when DG visited us, he had a middle-aged guy with him. "Dr. Lonappan," DG introduced him. He is our new medical officer."

We came to be very well acquainted. He lived in the Doctor's bungalow with his wife. His three children- all girls, were in boarding schools. He was a veteran plantation doctor and had been working in a tea estate in a smaller company.

"Here they are giving a much better salary, but what I can't stand is the climate. It was much cooler in tea," he complained. To compensate, he would take frequent tub baths, filling the tub with cold water and lots of ice cubes.

His work in the hospital was for just two hours in the morning and another two hours in the evening. His weaknesses were eggs and alcohol. He would have a dozen eggs every day, starting with a double bull's-eye with the bed coffee. Alcohol would have to wait till after the evening OP, but the lost time would be made up by night.

"I don't understand your psychology Thomas, slaving away like this for peanuts as compensation." He was right. His salary was more than double of what Jessy and I were earning together.

"But wouldn't it be boring? What will you do to pass time?"

"With a bottle in hand, nothing can be boring! And the money will be handy for educating our kids."

We got to meet very often. Finally, we had a doctor and family for company. It was good to discuss cases with another medical man. He was impressed by the range of cases we were managing.

19. Where Sita Returned to the Womb of Mother Earth

I was surprised to see CKM in the morning OP. He was looking sick. Since getting the company of Dr. Lonappan, I have not been regular at his place. It had been a while since we met.

"I have come to get admitted, Doctor. I have not been well for a week now. The pain and swelling in my thigh has recurred. The antibiotics that Dr. K. M. Thomas prescribed over phone doesn't seem to be working. I called him again today and he asked me to get admitted here. He will call you."

I saw that his thigh was swollen, warm, and red. He was running a high temperature. I admitted him and decided to wait for the call from Dr. Thomas. The call came through in the evening. I apprised him of CKM's condition.

"Start him on Amikacin," he advised. "Give a high dose- 750 milligrams morning and evening."

Amikacin was a new antibiotic that I had never used before. I told him so.

"That is the only feasible option, I think. Just regularly monitor his kidney function."

The drug was brought from Pathanamthitta and started on CKM. By the third day, he started improving. Dr. K. M. Thomas had advised for it to be given for seven days. By the fifth day, CKM was again feeling sick and nauseated. His urine became yellow and I noticed that he was jaundiced. I felt tense. I was not sure what caused his jaundice. *It really is quite stressful, treating your own friends or relatives.* I requested him to shift to Dr. K. M. Thomas's hospital in Kochi.

They left for Kochi in the afternoon. CKM was admitted there for another week. He returned, cured. "Amikacin is not known to have liver toxicity," Dr. Thomas had told him. "This might have been a rare occurrence, considering the high dose which was given."

Onam being the greatest festival of all Malayalees, the rush at the hospital came down significantly as we approached the day. We had just a few in-patients left, all of them quite stable. "I wish we could go somewhere for a change," I told CKM. He was now as healthy as ever. "It is now about two years since we have gone anywhere as a family. But wherever we go, we have to get back by nightfall."

"Divakaran Sir has asked me several times to visit him at his house one day, and bring you also along. He lives near Seethakuzhi, and the place is in the midst of dense forests."

"Seethakuzhi? Meaning, Seetha's pit? Why is it called that?"

"That is the place where Sita is supposed to have gone down into the earth. You can actually see the spot," CKM explained.

"I don't know if I will be able to make it. There are three in-patients now. Onam is a holiday for the hospital, so we don't have regular OP on that day. I'll see if things work out."

On the day just before Onam, as I wound up the evening OP, I was disappointed that there was one patient still admitted. She was having typhoid fever, and had been admitted three days back. She seemed to be responding to treatment, but still had occasional fever spikes. There was no way I could go out, keeping the patient here. Just then, a young guy sporting a large curled up moustache and an arrogant look, walked in.

"Doctor, tomorrow is Onam and you want to keep my mother here?"

"Actually I don't want to keep her here," I said. "But what else can I do? She is still weak and having fever off and on."

"You have been treating her for three days and still could not cure her?"

"Of course! Typhoid fever is not easily cured, especially since you had kept her home for more than a week with high fever, before bringing her to the hospital." I matched his aggression.

"I want to take her elsewhere for treatment," he declared.

His words were like music to my ears. *I will be able to take the day off tomorrow!*

"Please do," I said before he could change his mind. "I will also give you a fifty percent discount on your bill."

I couldn't wait to reach CKM's place. I dialed him from the hospital. "The last patient is being discharged now. Can we make the trip tomorrow?"

"Great! Divakaran Sir is here right now. Come over quick. We will decide everything."

We decided to hire a jeep and set off at 9 o'clock next day, ride through the forest paths and have lunch at Divakaran Sir's place. Jessy was exuberant, and it seemed that Aju also was sensing our excitement.

The Jeep arrived and we were about to get in, when there was a call from the hospital. It was a woman in labor! Feeling hopes of a getaway fading, I reluctantly went to examine the patient. It was a first pregnancy. On vaginal examination, I could see that, it was a breech presentation. The baby was lying upside down from the normal- the head was up and it was the buttocks poised to come out first. There was much more time left to full progression. We have done breech deliveries before, but this was not the day for an extended vigil.

"This won't be a normal sort of delivery. It will be a difficult one. It will be better if you take her to a higher centre," I hopefully tried to convince the relatives. They were relatively well off, and agreed to take her to Pathanamthitta.

I rushed back home where Jessy and Aju were waiting beside the jeep. "Come on, get in. We are going!"

Having picked up CKM and family, we set out. We had already entered the forest when someone noticed that in my rush, I had forgotten to put back my stethoscope. It was still slung around my neck. "The animals in the forest might think that a doctor has come to examine them," CKM's son joked.

The driver slammed the brakes so hard that we all fell forward. "Look! I nearly rammed into them!" he exclaimed. There were about eight to ten of them. Big, fat, wild boars. We were to see many more on the way. I became worried about Jessy, now in her seventh month. *This will be the worst place to have a miscarriage.* I asked him to go slower.

The driver stopped the vehicle after a while and drew our attention to a large jackfruit tree. "Giant squirrels!" There were three of them, feasting on a large fruit, unmindful of our presence. Each one was more than the size of a large rabbit. Their backs shone a fiery red as the sun beamed on them.

At another spot, he again stopped and pointed to the top of a hill. We could see nothing but what seemed like twigs sticking out from the tall grass. "Those are Sambar deer. Keep watching those twigs. They are its ears. You will see them when they raise their heads." Sure enough, one of them looked up, and we could see its head and long neck. As if on cue, the others also raised their heads. There were dozens of them.

As we continued, we saw peacocks, wild fowl, porcupines, and deer with long antlers. The highlight was when we reached a clearing near Seethakuzhi. It was a whole herd of elephants with three calves- one so tiny and cute. "It must be less than a month old," the driver commented. CKM and I got down for a closer look. "Don't go too near," he warned. "Herds don't usually attack, but you can't know when there are calves with them." The herd however decided that we were too close for comfort, and retreated into the trees.

Riding down a steep incline, we reached the river bank. We were at a spot a little further down from a small waterfall. The water was shallow. Just a few meters from the waterfall was the actual spot in the river bed through which Sita was supposed to have been sucked down into mother earth. The gorge itself could not be seen- being covered with water, but the churning of the water at its opening indicated the spot.

"It is a very narrow hole just wide enough for the slim Sita to go through. Nobody knows the depth." The driver was relaxing at the bank, leaning on his jeep. "If you unfurl a spool of thread with a stone tied at the end, you won't be able to reach the bottom."

I looked around and broke off a long branch from a fallen tree. It was about twenty feet long. I pushed it down into the abyss, as far as it would go. There was no resistance. I let go of it, and it just got sucked down, disappearing from sight. I wished I had brought a spool of thread.

Divakaran Sir's house was right in the middle of the forest. It was a moderately large and well furnished house, the only one around. We had seen only some makeshift huts on the way, occupied by tribals. Of course, there was no electricity.

Sir showed us around. There were some huge rosewood trees within his compound. "Each one can fetch over a hundred thousand rupees," he informed us. "But we are not allowed to cut it. Even damaging any one of them will be a great offence."

"How come you got this property right in the middle of the forest?" I was curious.

"I have the proper title deeds for it," he said flatly. I thought it best not to probe further.

Before lunch, Divakaran Sir served us the local brew- Arrack. "It is the best quality, brewed with ayurvedic herbs," he explained as he poured me a full glass.

'Wait, I don't think I can have that much. I will go slowly."

"Okay, then help yourself," he said, giving me an empty glass. He took the full glass and pinching his nostrils shut with his left hand, he gulped down the liquor in one go.

I sipped from the small amount I had poured myself. I could feel it burning down all the way to my stomach. "I need water!" I gasped. I grabbed the glass brought quickly to me by his wife and gulped it down. The burning soothed a little. I had the rest of the drink slowly and diluted generously with water.

"You are spoiling the drink!" Divakaran Sir was scornful. He took another full glass for himself and poured it down his throat just as before.

There was plenty of fried meat and boiled tapioca to go with the drink. I had never tasted meat that tasty, ever in my life. "Its wild boar," his wife explained. "Sir won't eat or drink anything without it as accompaniment."

True to her word, he was mouthing the pieces of meat without a pause. I was reminded of Obelix. Come to think of it, he looked very much like the comic character. Other than the fact that his long hair was black and not braided like Obelix's, Sir resembled him exactly with his bulbous nose, puffed out cheeks and pot belly.

My head reeled from the drink. By the time lunch was over, my stomach was on the verge of bursting. Divakaran Sir seemed to notice my discomfort. "Why don't you lie down and rest for some time, Doctor?" I didn't need a second invitation.

After my nap, we had some tea. I declined the offer of another drink. On reaching back, I was relieved to know that there were no emergencies that had come during our absence. None of us wanted dinner, and we retired early.

Though we had been gone for only eight hours and travelled less than thirty kilometers, I felt I had been on a long vacation.

20. A Murderer in Our Bedroom!

It was raining heavily the whole night. I woke up and walked to the kitchen to make a coffee and was surprised to see a pool of water in the corridor. A ray of light was shining from above. I looked up to see a couple of roof tiles were missing. Could the wind have blown them off? But there had not been that much wind!

Coming back to the bedroom with the coffee, I noticed the wooden shelf was wide open with the drawer also pulled out. I looked inside. The money kept there- the previous day's collection from the hospital, was missing. Frantic, I searched the pockets of my shirt hung on the cloth stand, where I usually kept my personal cash. That too was missing. My wristwatch which had been on the table was also gone.

"We have been robbed!" I exclaimed to Jessy. "I'll go and report to the police station." I started my bike and set off, but the bike choked to a halt after a few meters. Puzzled, I checked and found the petrol tank empty. I had filled it up just two days ago. The thief seemed to have drained out the petrol too!

Keeping the bike on its stand by the side of the road, I walked to CKM. There was a shop which sold petrol in cans. The price was ten percent higher, and it would be adulterated with kerosene. Anyhow, I didn't have a single penny on me to buy it.

"Did you inform the police?" CKM asked.

"I was going to. But the bike stopped midway. The thief seems to have drained off the petrol, and I don't have any cash with me. You will have to lend me some."

"Call them from here," he said as he gave me three hundred rupees and a can for buying petrol.

It was Sunny who answered the phone. "We will be there right now. Don't disturb anything."

They took a detailed statement from me. Inspecting all around the house, they found a footprint on a ledge on the wall of the kitchen. He must have climbed on to the roof, removed those tiles, got down into the corridor and walked straight into our bedroom! Our bedroom door's latch had long been dysfunctional.

A week went by, and there was no progress in the investigation. We made sure to always bolt the door of the corridor at night. Early in the morning, Jessy shook me awake. "The thief came again last night," she informed me.

"What? When? How do you know?!"

She described how she had woken up in the night on hearing a grinding sound. Looking out through the door of the bedroom, she could make out the silhouette of a man against the window of the corridor. He seemed to be sawing through the wooden check grail of the window.

"But then, why didn't you wake me up?"

She had calculated that it was almost dawn, and the thief would not have managed to saw through and get in before light. "Knowing you, I know you would have rushed to confront him. What if he were carrying a knife?"

I could only marvel at her infinite wisdom!

We opened the door of the corridor and saw that the roof tiles had been removed again. There was a towel hung on the rail of the window where he was standing. We removed it to see that he had tried to cover the area where he had tried to saw through the wood, with the towel. He probably left it incomplete, seeing that dawn was breaking.

I set out again for the police station. This time, he had not stolen petrol.

Sunny was greatly disturbed. "We must get this guy. He seems to be getting bolder!"

There was panic at both my parents' and in-laws' place. "You have to reconsider staying there. It seems like a dangerous place," my mother-in-law wrote.

I made it a habit to keep a heavy wooden stick by the side of the bed at night. I finally gave up my habit of keeping all my cash in my shirt pocket. Sunny deployed policemen to patrol the vicinity at night. An emergency meeting of the local committee was conveyed. This time, they were worried that we might decide to leave for good.

"This house is not safe," the vicar told the members. "Anyone can get in by removing some of the roof tiles." It was decided to put a false ceiling below the roof with a wooden grid and asbestos sheets. All the doors were to be fitted with proper latches. "No thief will be able to get in easily, and it will be cooler for you inside the rooms." They also decided to write off the amount lost from the hospital's collection.

I got a phone call from Sunny while I was in the morning OP. "We have nabbed a man roaming around your house at midnight. While accosting him, he tried to make a run for it, but our policemen caught him. We are questioning him now."

I knew how the police would question. It would be more physical than verbal! "I hope someone innocent is not harmed," I said.

Sunny visited me at home in the evening. "It's him, Doctor. We have caught the right guy."

"How can you be sure?"

"He has confessed everything." Seeing my skeptical look, he continued. "Of course, our methods are different from Scotland Yard's. We beat the hell out of him and get a confession!"

"But then, won't he just confess to avoid torture?"

"Tomorrow, I will lay rest to your doubts. I will be bringing him to your house to get the details."

He was brought in handcuffs by two policemen. Some more details were now known about him. He was actually a murder accused, out on bail. He had been charged with murdering his own mother and burying her under the floor of their house. *Jessy had been wise not to have woken me up that day!*

"Show us how you entered the house," a policeman ordered. Without hesitation, he walked to the back of the kitchen and showed the spot where he had stepped on the ledge on the wall to climb on the roof- the exact spot where we had seen his footprint. When asked to describe the interior of the house, he gave the correct layout of everything- including the drawer from where he had taken the money. He also showed where he had tried to cut through the check rail of the window on his second attempt. He had abandoned the effort, seeing that dawn was breaking.

"I am convinced," I admitted when Sunny called.

"We both might be convinced, but for a conviction to occur, we have to have more proof. His lawyer will argue that we have forced him to confess. I am going to Pathanamthitta now. I have got the address of the shop where he has sold your watch."

By evening, Sunny called me. "Please come to the station after your OP. I want you to identify the watch."

I confirmed the watch to be the one stolen from me.

"We now have the evidence we need. With his confession and other circumstantial evidence, we are sure to nail him!" Sunny was happy.

21. A Car and a Daughter

Jessy was advancing in her pregnancy. The due date was just two months away. She flatly refused my suggestion of having the delivery done here itself. "If something goes wrong, you might get upset and may find it difficult to handle the situation, this being your own child."

I didn't anticipate any problems or even if there were, I was confident of handling it. But I had to agree to her decision, though reluctantly. We applied for a maternity leave for three months, which was promptly sanctioned by Thirumeni.

With the arrival of another child, it will be difficult for Jessy to visit her parents once in a while, travelling by bus. I decided we needed a car. My brother arranged for a second hand Ambassador car. To pay for it, we cleaned up all the bank deposits we had, but it wouldn't suffice. I sold my bike and completed the payment. I had a sinking feeling on the day they came and took my bike away. It was like losing a member of the family.

CKM arranged a friend of his, an ex-driver from Saudi, to bring the car from Thiruvalla and then teach me to drive it. I went with him to take delivery of the vehicle. It was a jet black beautiful Mark3 Ambassador car. "It's a bargain at thirty thousand rupees," he remarked.

Each evening he would come to take me for driving lessons. CKM would sometimes accompany us. We usually drove through the roads to Sabarimala and often we would see wild animals on the way. Once I had driven all the way to the foothills of Sabarimala on my own, I felt confident. "Now you should get accustomed to driving in traffic. I will accompany you once to your house in Thiruvalla. After that, you should be on your own," my instructor declared.

"Why don't we visit your ancestral house in Pathanamthitta, instead?" CKM suggested. "I would love to see the place."

We went on a Sunday afternoon.

The house had been abandoned ever since my grandmother was taken rather forcefully to Thiruvalla by my father seven years back. She was past eighty then and living alone in the crumbling house. "It might be better to demolish the old house," my father had suggested, but I had opposed the idea. The happy vacations we spent there with all our cousins were a lingering nostalgia.

We had to park the car on the road and walk up to the house on a hill. The path was overgrown with weeds. Luckily, we had a machete with which we cleared a tract through which we could walk up. We peered through a broken window of the locked house and saw weeds growing high from the floor. Bats were hanging from the ceiling.

"If you work at it, you can redeem this house," CKM said. "It will be impossible to build a house like this - with the wooden ceiling and earthen roof tiles, in future. You should renovate it."

"It is my wish that I settle down here someday," I replied.

Soon after Jessy's parents took her and Aju to Thiruvalla, I began to feel lonely. I would wait impatiently for the evening to arrive so that I could go to CKM's place. The maid would have cooked my dinner which I would eat on returning. I found the food tasteless. It was the same maid who made the dishes earlier. Was it because I was eating it cold? I tried warming the food before eating, but it was the same. I realized that food tastes better in the company of near and dear ones.

The worst time was at night when I would be alone, not knowing what to do. The movie cassettes I took on rent didn't interest me. I found myself sometimes even wishing for a call from the hospital to break the monotony!

I made it a regular routine of going to Thiruvalla on alternate Sunday afternoons, to come back by evening on the same day. One trip in the car cost me almost a tenth of my monthly salary. The car would run nine kilometers for a liter of petrol. "Very good for an old Ambassador car," I was told. I missed my bike.

To save petrol, I switched to walking to CKM's place, but I found this option troublesome. Most people on the road would be my patients. They would start a detailed consultation on the road. As one parley was going on, there would be other patients waiting for their turn.

"This consultation on the road is not the proper way. Come to the hospital at OP time. There should be a proper examination and maybe some investigations," I would repeatedly say to deaf ears. I gave up walking and made my visit in the car itself limiting it to once or twice a week.

The patients as well as my staff seemed to be noticing a change in my mood. "Why are you so impatient with me now, Doctor? You were not like this earlier." Kunjamma had been a regular patient ever since the beginning. Hearing these words from her, I decided I needed to do something.

I dug up some painting materials we had brought from Trivandrum. I had planned to do some paintings but had never got around to it. It was years since I had painted anything. I got going with a vengeance. I would paint late into the night, stopping only when I felt too exhausted. Getting up in the morning, I would be disappointed with my work. The colors that I had painfully mixed and applied on the canvas at night under the glare of the bulb would seem very different and dull in daylight. Undaunted, I persisted.

Having painted large canvases with sceneries, I went on to portraits of Aju and Jessy. Loneliness didn't seem much of a problem anymore. In fact, it became a blessing.

One night, as I was giving the finishing touches on Jessy's portrait, Chackochan came with the news. "We got a call at the hospital, Doctor. Dr Jessy has given birth. It is a girl. Normal delivery. It was in the afternoon, but they could get the call through only now."

A boy and a girl! That's perfect!

Soon after morning OP the next day, I set out in my car. The little one was active. 'She looks just like her dad', was the universal opinion.

Jessy related to me the events. She was admitted early in the morning with pain. By noon, the pain had intensified and she felt the baby coming. She looked around, but there was no staff in sight. The lady in the adjacent bed, whose pain had just started, ran out to call the sister. By the time they arrived, the baby was already out and lying on the cot. Jessy also suffered a large vaginal tear.

"Such a thing would never have happened if you had the delivery in our hospital," I remarked.

"True," she agreed. "Our sisters are so sincere and vigilant."

I went to collect Jessy, Aju and the new addition to the family on a Sunday two weeks later. The bill at the hospital was above rupees two thousand and five hundred only. We don't charge even a fifth of this amount in our hospital for much greater care!

Aju was intrigued by seeing his and Jessy's portraits. "How did you take our photo when we were away?"

Once Jessy also started coming for work in the hospital after another month, I felt relieved of the strain. The young one was irritable with the maids when we were away at work but would quieten down when I reached home in the evening. I would carry her around singing lullabies. There was a song with the chorus going 'Cuckoodee, Cuckooda," which I often sang. She came to be called 'Cuckoo'.

Three weeks later, DG came visiting. He was alone. "I've come to say goodbye. I've been transferred."

We heard the news in shocked silence. "Where are you going, DG uncle?" Aju asked.

"I have to report at Punalur estate tomorrow. It is about eighty kilometers from here."

We exchanged our permanent addresses. "We will meet somewhere, someday, somehow," I said and bid him goodbye.

It was to be much sooner than any of us expected.

22. A Greater Thirumeni

Our facilities were becoming inadequate for the increasing number of patients. I felt bad when a regular patient coming with some acute illness had to be sent to Pathanamthitta just for want of a bed to admit him. The patients thus referred were very upset. 'We have been coming here regularly, and when we really need it, you are sending us away.'

I apprised Thirumeni about the situation. "We will need a new building," I wrote. "The hospital has savings of 1.5 lakhs in the bank. If we take a loan and go ahead with the construction, we can easily pay the installments from our monthly income."

Thirumeni was supportive. "Get an engineer to make a plan and estimate," he wrote. The local committee members also were enthusiastic. An engineer was roped in. We had detailed discussions. Finally, we had a plan ready for a three-story building with ample space for twenty more beds, a proper labor room, a small ICU, and an operation theatre.

I also felt the need for training to take up more complicated cases and major surgeries. It was around this time that we came to know of a new post-graduate course for general practitioners, being started by Vellore Medical College. It was precisely for upgrading the skills of doctors working in rural areas. The duration of the course was for four years. There should be a sponsoring agency that needs the doctor's services and they should pay a stipend for the doctor during his training. The doctors thus selected should give a bond to serve them for four years.

Jessy bravely volunteered to manage the hospital alone, till I finished the course. "Submit your application. If you are selected, we will work things out." Thirumeni was informed, and he gave the go-ahead.

I was on cloud nine. Enquiries had suggested that I would most probably be selected since I was already working in a remote rural area. By the time I finish my studies and acquire new skills, the new building would be complete and we would be setting up a major hospital with all the basic facilities needed for that area. Of course, it would be a major challenge for us, with me being alone and away from the family for four years, and Jessy having to manage the hospital on her own. But we were firm in our resolution to overcome all obstacles.

Summer that year was particularly harsh. The well dried up completely. We spent a large amount of money for deepening the well, blasting the rock on the floor with dynamite, but got no result. It was impossible for Chackochan to fetch enough water for all the needs. The water level in Pappychayan's well had also gone down. If we continue to draw water from there, they will also be facing a shortage.

We built a ground-level tank in front of the hospital building and engaged a water tanker lorry to fetch water from the river. We purchased a small motor to pump water from there to the overhead tank. The problem was solved, but we had to incur an additional cost of two hundred rupees every day.

It was in early April of 1989, that I received the bombshell- a letter from Thirumeni. As part of reorganizing the Church administration, the Kottayam diocese was bifurcated and a new diocese, the Ranni-Nilackal diocese, created. It will be governed by a much senior bishop, His Grace Joseph Mar Osthathiose. Since the hospital comes under his jurisdiction, I was to report to him hither forth.

Nilackal was a burning issue which started in the early eighties, even threatening the unique religious harmony which existed in Kerala. A stone cross was unearthed in a farm at the foothills of the Sabarimala Temple, and was promptly declared as the one which St. Thomas himself had planted there a thousand and nine hundred years ago. Many locals spoke of the role of a scheming Christian priest having cunningly buried an old stone cross to be 'discovered' and dug up later. An agitation was started demanding a church at the spot. Many suspected their motivation. Since Sabarimala temple was raking in money, a church along the route would be able to take in a share of the bounty. Hindu organizations began a counter agitation. A peaceful end was finally agreed upon, with government arbitration. The Nilackal Church came up, a little further away from the main route to Sabarimala. Our church too had a share of the pie, and thus, the Ranni-Nilackal Diocese was created.

I felt devastated, feeling I had lost my mentor. But maybe it will be for the good. Valiya Thirumeni (Valiya meaning big or great, added to the title considering his senior status) was a well-known figure even outside the church. He was known as the bishop with the golden tongue. He was an excellent orator, interlacing his powerful speeches with lots of wit and humor.

I still remembered one of his speeches given at the Maramon convention, one of the largest Christian gatherings in the world, on the banks of the Pamba river. He was speaking on the necessity of having a proper foundation in life. The metaphor he gave for stressing his message was classic.

'A young English lady visiting Kerala wished to wear a sari. A group of local young women volunteered to help, but the sari would not remain in place despite trying for a long time. Finally, an old woman identified the basic problem. The lady was not wearing an underskirt to secure the sari at her waist!'

In a way, the change may be to our advantage. Being very senior and high in the hierarchy of the church, he might be able to make bold decisions. And Ranny being much closer to Chittar, access to him also might be easier. Still, I would miss the support and the benign benevolence of Zacharias Thirumeni.

Soon I received the news that Valia Thirumeni will be visiting the Chittar parish. The Vicar came to meet me. "After the church service, we are arranging lunch for him at your quarters. It is the most convenient place. Is it okay for you?"

"Of course, it will be a pleasure," I replied.

"He will take a rest at your place after lunch. In the evening, we will have a short meeting of the local committee, before he leaves for a public meeting. Please arrange a room where he can rest, and keep a toilet clean for his use."

Preparation for his visit started two days early. Pappychayan was recruited for the preparation of the fish curry. Jessy volunteered to prepare the other dishes.

The vicar informed me that there will be fourteen people. "There will be many accompanying him. There will also be important members of the church."

Valiya Thirumeni enjoyed the lunch. "The fish curry is superb!" he complimented my wife.

"But that was prepared by Pappychayan," she informed. Pappychayan was not among the invitees.

Everyone departed after lunch, leaving Valiya Thirumeni to take rest.

Aju went to his room and was talking to him.

"Come here Aju," I called him. "Let Thirumeni have some rest."

"Let him be, Doctor," Valiya Thirumeni interrupted. "I am enjoying our conversation."

Over tea, we discussed the hospital. "You should have peripheral services. You must visit the patient's houses and provide primary care," he advised.

I tried to explain to him that patients came here from very far off places. "We are tied up with the work in the hospital, which receives even serious patients. If we are to go out visiting houses, work at the hospital will go haywire."

"We have a tie-up with an agency in Japan. I will send you there for the training." He didn't go into any specifics.

I told him about the course in Vellore and about our plans to construct a new building. He was noncommittal. "Let the local committee decide. But you should plan to continue here for a long time."

"Once my children are old enough to go to school, it might be difficult for us. We might have to put them in boarding schools," I said.

"We should also start a school. That way, you won't have any problem." His ideas seemed grandiose and impractical. I found myself resenting his patronizing attitude.

The local committee meeting was brief, as Valia Thirumeni had to leave for the public meeting. We presented the accounts of the hospital. I mentioned our increased daily expenses on account of ferrying water from the river.

"That is a sheer waste!" Valiya Thirumeni declared, before getting up to leave. "Stop that practice today itself. I will send a team to dig a bore well."

"But how will we manage until the work on the bore well is complete?" I wondered soon after he left.

"Let Chackochen fetch water for a few days from the neighbors till we get the borewell done," one of the members opined.

A week went by and there was no sign of any bore well diggers. All activities needing water had to be stopped. There was no mopping of the floors or cleaning of the toilets. Only water essential for drinking and washing were supplied to the patients. They started to complain, and the number of inpatients declined.

Still, it became difficult to provide adequate water. If it goes on like this, we will have to close down the hospital! Already, I had sent two reminders to Valia Thirumeni. I received no reply. Twelve days after his visit, a team arrived to check the feasibility of a bore well. They left very soon. The hospital building was straight across the property, there was no way to take a tractor to the back, and the cable would not reach there from the road.

I decided to wait no more. Not waiting for Thirumeni's instructions, we resumed the earlier practice of transporting water from the river. We continued it till the rain replenished the water in the well by June.

One evening, Dr. Lonappan turned up with the new Asst. Manager who had come in place of DG. They had a formal agenda.

"Our company's medical officer in Punalur estate has been terminated. Our manager has asked us to get you to apply for the job," the Asst. Manager informed.

"It will be good for you," Dr. Lonappan added. Punalur is a much larger estate than Chittar with many more facilities. The estate hospital has six beds for inpatients. The town is not very far, and it has got good schools and hospitals. You can all stay in the nice doctor's bungalow there. The school bus from town comes to the estate. Jessy also can work in any of the private hospitals in town."

"All this sounds good," I agreed. "But what about this hospital? Won't it get shut down yet again?"

"I think you are suffering from a Messiah Complex, Thomas." Dr.

Lonappan was frank. "You should get out of it."

"I'll think about it," I promised.

It was now more than three months since we had completed our second year in the hospital but there was no word from the Diocesan office about our annual increment or the earned leave payment of a month's salary usually given each year. I wrote to Valiya Thirumeni about this but didn't get a response even after two weeks.

In the next local committee meeting, I did some frank speaking. "You all know that we are working for a salary way below what is being paid for the junior doctors working in the town hospitals. I have decided not to let myself be exploited thus. I have decided to leave. Please find some other doctor to carry on the work here."

My announcement was met with shocked silence. "Doctor, don't make a hasty decision. We will contact Valiya Thirumeni and get a favorable decision next week," the Vicar pleaded.

Next week, I got a letter from the Diocese informing me that a committee has been formed to study our salary revision.

23. A Narrow Save

It was Lakshmi's second delivery at the hospital. The first one was completely normal and was just one and a half years back. "It is a bit too early to have conceived another child," I had told her when she came for a check-up. The size of the uterus was quite large, but it didn't seem to be twins.

Since she didn't have any periods after her last pregnancy, it was quite late when this one was detected. By the time she had come for the check-up, it was already advanced by seven months. Routine tests showed her blood sugar was above normal. "Pregnancy-induced diabetes," I told her. She was started on daily insulin and it was brought under control. The delivery was uneventful although the baby turned out to be 3.8 kilograms.

I was preparing to leave when I noticed that blood was oozing out from the vagina in much larger quantities than normal. I pressed over the abdomen, and large red clots gushed out and got splattered all over the place.

I felt for the uterus. It was soft and flabby. It should have been as hard as a cricket ball by now. "Quick! Methergine and Pitocin injections!"

While the drugs were given, I vigorously massaged the uterus trying to carouse it to contract, but it remained soft and flabby. The blood was flowing out as if from a bucket! Pushing in IV fluids and grasping the uterus tight in my hand, I pushed in several meters of sterile gauze tight into the uterus.

Thankfully, Lakshmi was still conscious, though worried. "We have to get her fast to another hospital!" I told her parents who were waiting outside with the baby. "I will bring my own car." I knew it would take them some time to arrange another vehicle.

I drove at breakneck speed with the headlights on. Lakshmi was lying on the back seat, her legs raised onto her father's lap as I had advised. Her mother sat in the front, holding the baby. The Ranny Mission Hospital was run by the same church denomination as ours. They had full-time gynecologists and operation theatre facilities.

"Postpartum hemorrhage!" I quickly told the lady doctor in casualty. "BP is low."

"TTT! How are you dear?"

I recognized the doctor as Mina, my classmate at Medical College. We had been together in the Music club also. She had been the best female singer in our class.

"We will talk later," I said. "The patient is bad. Her BP is too low!"

The gynecologist was called in. "Take her immediately to the theatre," she ordered and scrambled after the trolley. I waited in the casualty, talking to Mina.

She was married to an engineer, and they were living at his house which was nearby. We talked about old times. I wished I could hear her singing again, but this casualty was certainly not the ideal place. We switched topics to our present situation. She was fascinated by our work in Chittar.

"I would never have imagined you would be working in a place like Chittar! Wonderful, that you are managing such difficult cases there." I explained how I would be forced to, many a time by the patients.

"How is your work here?"

"It's okay, TT. I have to work six days a week, nine to five. There are five junior doctors like me, so I will have night duty once every five days. On those days, I don't have to come in the day and I will get the next day off."

"Seems like you are having quite a relaxed job here. Do you have any other leaves? And may I ask you how much they pay you?"

"Certainly, TT. Why have you to ask so formally? I get three thousand rupees a month. We have twelve days of casual leave and another twelve days as annual leave each year."

For working less than a fifth of what I had to do, she was earning more! That too, without any major responsibility. Specialists were there to take care of all the difficult cases.

Just then, the Medical Superintendent of the hospital, Dr. John came in. I have had several phone conversations with him, but was meeting him for the first time.

"Doctor, you are here? I was looking for you. They have taken up that case for surgery. We will have to remove the uterus. There was no way we could stop the bleeding otherwise. Anyway, it is not much of an issue, now that she is already having two children."

"I was talking to Mina here. We were classmates. We were reliving our memories."

"Oho..You may have a lot to talk about!" He glanced at my feet. "Doctor, your trousers and feet are all covered in blood! My residence is just adjacent. Come with me and wash up."

Having washed off the blood as best as I could, I sat down and accepted the tea he offered. "How is the hospital doing?" I asked as one medical superintendent to another, even though mine was a tiny setup compared to his.

"We are just okay. There are patients coming, but after paying all the salaries and other expenses, we are not able to break even. The church subsidizes us for the shortfall."

"But it seems you are paying a good salary, from what I learned from Dr. Mina."

"We are paying just the bare minimum. Which doctor will come and work for less?"

"You know what work I am doing there. We are on duty 24/7. Do you know my salary is less than that, though the hospital is making a surplus?"

Dr. John looked me straight in the eye. "Doctor, you should understand that the church has no qualms about exploiting those who let themselves be exploited."

We returned to the hospital. "The surgery is over, and she is fine," the gynecologist informed us. Turning to me, she exclaimed. "You seem to have the best of patients! Rarely will you get a patient in such distress, so calm and co-operative! Would you like to see her?"

I was led to the post-operative room. Lakshmi was drowsy from the sedation, but she gave a faint smile. "I'm okay, Doctor. Thank you so much."

Back home, I noticed the dried bloodstains all over the back seat of my car. *I will get Chackochan also to help, and clean it later.*

*****

In the evening OP, I had two surprise visitors- Sally and Johnykutty! Both looked happy and content and somewhat matured. After the pleasantries, Johnykutty told me the real purpose of their visit.

"It's a week since Sally has missed her periods. Is she pregnant?"

The pregnancy test was positive. Both seemed excited. I ordered the other routine investigations and sent them with instructions to come for regular follow-ups.

24. The Bishop's Palace

The prospectus and application form arrived from Vellore. I filled up the form carefully. The last column was for the sponsoring agency. It had to be signed by the responsible person agreeing to pay a stipend for the student throughout the period of the course. The proposal for the new building also was pending. I decided to go and meet Valia Thirumeni at his office. The Vicar agreed to fix up an appointment, and accompany me to Ranny.

The meeting was scheduled for 11 am on a Saturday. We arrived five minutes early. The Bishop's Palace was in a sprawling compound away from the town. Hectic work was in progress. The building was being renovated with new flooring and fresh paint, and a new block was being built as an extension. It would house the new reception area, the bishop's office, and his residence. The old building was to be converted into an office complex. The compound was strewn with large slabs of marble and granite, and bustling with laborers hard at work.

"You will have to wait for some time. Valia Thirumeni is in a discussion with some delegates from the Church of England," his personal assistant informed us. We sat in the waiting room. *I should have brought a book to read.* We could hear loud laughter from inside. Thirumeni must be at his witty best. Finally, we were ushered in at quarter past twelve. The young, foreign couple who took leave of Valiya Thirumeni were still smiling, full of mirth.

"It will be time for Valia Thirumeni to take lunch soon. Please keep your meeting short," the assistant warned us.

Valiya Thirumeni welcomed us in. "So what news in Chittar?" he asked. The room was aesthetically furnished. On one corner was a large traditional grinding stone.

'Why is this here?" the Vicar asked puzzled. "We keep this in the kitchen."

"For the same reason as to why that is kept there," Valiya Thirumeni smiled, pointing to a large wooden elephant kept in the opposite corner. "Only in areas like Chittar, you have such things in the kitchen. In other places, people use electric mixie and grinder."

I was not very amused at the way the discussion was going on about grinding stones and mixies, especially since we had been warned about the shortage of time. I came straight to the point.

"We have prepared a plan for a new building. We are not able to cater to all the patients now with the present set up. The plan and estimate have already been sent to you. We will have to take a loan to complete it and will need the church to stand as guarantor.

"How can we pay back such a huge amount?" Valiya Thirumeni was skeptical.

"The present income in the hospital itself is enough to pay the monthly installment of about rupees ten thousand. We can complete the work in one two or three years. Meanwhile, if you sponsor my training, I can complete the course and come back to work with enhanced skills. We will be able to start surgeries and manage patients needing intensive care. There will be increased income."

"But how can we be sure that you will stay and work here till this loan is paid back?"

"See Thirumeni," I started to explain a bit impatiently. "We have been working there for two and a half years without any obligation, in spite of better options in the urban centers. Why would you doubt our commitment? Moreover, the condition for joining the course is that I have to execute a bond for four years."

"But four years is not enough to repay the loan." Valiya Thirumeni seemed difficult to convince.

"See Thirumeni, we are now working even without any bond. Our ambition is to build up this hospital and solve the shortage of medical facilities in that area. Actually, we plan to spend our whole life there."

"It is difficult for the church to take up such a huge financial burden. Anyway, I don't want to make a decision on my own. I will present these ideas at the next Diocesan Council. We will make a decision there."

"But the application for the course has to reach Vellore within two weeks." I paused for a moment and posed the question that was nagging in my mind. "How can this be a big burden for the church? The money that has to be borrowed will not even come to anywhere near the amount you are now spending here to build up the Bishop's Palace."

Valiya Thirumeni gave me a sharp look. Bishops are not used to being talked back like that. Even the Vicar seemed shocked.

Thirumeni's secretary came in. "It is time for Valiya Thirumeni to have his lunch break. I hope your business is over."

He must have been listening in to our discussion and probably not pleased with the direction it was going!

We left soon. "I will look into your suggestions," Thirumeni had promised.

The letter from Valiya Thirumeni arrived just two days before I was to submit the application to Vellore. I opened it eagerly.

Dear Dr. Thomas and Dr. Jessy,

Greetings to you in the name of our Lord, Jesus Christ.

The Diocesan Council was convened and has extensively discussed the proposals submitted by you. It was felt that the construction of a new building for the hospital can be taken up later, once the hospital has enough funds to finance at least fifty percent of the project. The church can stand guarantee for the rest of the amount, for which a loan can be taken.

Regarding the course in Vellore, we are glad to allow you to join the course, for which we will be happy to sponsor you. You will be given leave for four years, after which you should rejoin duty. Dr. Jessy should manage the hospital as Medical Superintendent during your absence. She will be given a ten percent increase in her salary for the extra work during this period. Both of you should give an undertaking in writing, agreeing to the above terms.

As there is no precedence of the church bearing the stipend of any student, you should bear the expenses of your education on your own.

Hope this letter finds you in the best of physical, mental, and spiritual health.

Yours in His name,

Signed

Dr. Joseph Mar Osthathios

Suffragan Metropolitan in charge,

Ranni-Nilackal Diocese.

I handed the letter to Jessy. Her face fell as she read through the contents. "How can we bear the expenses here as well as for your studies there with just my salary?"

"Of course it is impossible!" I said taking the letter back from her and going through it again. "And if we are to build up half of the money for the new building, it will take at least four years, by which time, the cost might be double the present estimate. If they are not interested in improving the hospital, why should we be bothered?" I responded dismissively. But I was seething inside. *He seems to think that we were working here for our own necessity, not getting a job elsewhere!* I crumpled up the letter and threw it into the dustbin.

25. Another Illegitimate Birth

Dawn was just breaking when Sr. Mariamma herself came rushing to my house. "Doctor! Come quickly! A girl has given birth to a baby in our bathroom!"

"Which girl? Which bathroom?" I rushed after her, not even bothering to change from my lungi and T-shirt.

"We don't know, Doctor, none of us have seen this girl before. She is not answering any questions. She delivered in the common bathroom attached to the general ward." Sister Mariamma was panting harder than me.

The girl was sitting on the floor of the bathroom with her sari up. The child lay beside her, on the floor, the umbilical cord connecting them.

"Bring the delivering set!" I shouted and lifted the baby onto her lap. I put two adjacent ties on the cord and cut between them. I handed the baby to the sister. "Clean it up and cover it with warm clothes, then help this girl into the labor room."

One of the patients in the ward donated some clean rags in which the baby was wrapped snugly. A quick examination showed no problems with the baby. I tried to gently pull on the cord and take out the placenta. It was not moving. I tried putting my whole hand into the uterus to try and dislodge it, but the cervix- the outlet of the uterus- was already closed tight. Pulling hard on the cord might cause the whole uterus to get inverted and come out. That would be a catastrophe!

I knew I had to get her to a hospital where the placenta could be removed after dilating the cervix under anesthesia. "When did she give birth? The cervix seems already closed."

"We have no idea, Doctor. We came to know only when some of the patients in the ward alerted us. They were woken up from their sleep by the sound of a baby crying."

The girl just lay there. She seemed unconcerned about anything. "Now stop fooling and answer me! Who are you? When did you deliver this child?" I shouted at her. She just smiled back. *Is she insane?* "Keep a watch on her, and make her breastfeed the baby, I told Sister. "I will be back."

Rushing home and changing to more presentable attire, I got into my car and drove swiftly to the police station. I met Sunny at his quarters and apprised him of the situation.

"Okay, you can get back to the hospital, Doctor. We will be there soon. I will send the ASI (The Assistant Sub Inspector)."

By the time I got back, the nurses had extracted some information from her. Her name was Aswathy. She seemed to be mentally retarded or abnormal. She used to roam around and has slept with several men, so the paternity of the child was anybody's guess. Her parents were living eight kilometers away, on the fringe of the forest. They had expelled her from their home some years back and had no contact with her since.

The police jeep arrived with three policemen, including the driver and the ASI. I was relieved to see them. "We have to get her to the government hospital in Pathanamthitta quickly. With the placenta still inside, she may develop complications any moment," I said.

"We will take her in the jeep," the ASI volunteered. "But you also have to come with us, to inform them of the details."

"But Sir, the hospital will not accept a patient without an attendant. They might ask the Doctor or one of us to stay back with her," the other policeman spoke up.

The ASI thought for a moment. "Get that girl and her child into the jeep. We will go to her parent's house first."

The parents were astonished to see the police arrive at their hut. The father was busy milking their cow.

"We can't come with you. And we don't have such a daughter!" The man looked up impatiently.

"You'd better!" The ASI's voice was threatening. "Otherwise, if anything happens to her, we will file a case against you and you will have to go to jail." The poor couple had no option. The husband quickly finished milking and entrusted its further care to the neighbors while his wife packed up a few things, and both meekly got into the jeep.

The doctor on duty in the casualty was a forensic surgeon. "This is obviously a medico-legal case," he observed. "We need to record your statement."

"Show the lady to the gynecologist on duty," he ordered the nurse, and went on to write down my detailed statement. We were interrupted by the nurse.

"Sir, the gynecologist wants to take up the patient immediately for placenta removal under anesthesia. She wants a bottle of blood to be arranged. Her group is A positive."

"Check the blood group of her parents. One of them might match."

"We have already checked them, Sir. They don't match. One is O positive and the other, B positive."

The casualty doctor and I exchanged meaningful looks and smiled at each other. So this girl herself was most likely an illegitimate product! None of the others present could make out what the joke was between us.

"I am A positive. I can donate," I ventured.

"But you are looking tired. Let them find someone else."

"But who else? The parents are O positive and B positive." We once again exchanged a smirk. "There is no one else with them. It's okay. I was a regular donor during my student days."

I was taken to the cubicle for draining blood. I lay down, the needle was inserted into my arm, and the blood started flowing into the collection bottle. After some time, I felt somewhat light-headed, and then began sweating profusely. Alarmed, the nurse rushed to call the doctor.

"Stop the bleeding and start an IV fluid," he ordered while checking my BP. "Your BP is too low. I thought you said you had been a regular donor?"

"It's just that I've had nothing to eat today," I replied. I just remembered that leave alone food, I haven't even had my regular morning cup of coffee!

"Why didn't you tell me earlier? I wouldn't have taken your blood!" He bent down to inspect the bottle. "We have 300ml. That is enough for now. Let them start the surgery. In case more is needed, we'll transfuse from the O positive parent. And take this doctor to my resting room once the IV fluid is finished. Let him lie there and take rest."

I woke up much later, hearing the doctor entering the room. "I have brought lunch for both of us. We'll have it here together." He placed two packets on the table. "The surgery is over and the girl is fine."

We talked about our different areas of work over lunch. "Being the police surgeon, I am not actually bound to do casualty duty. But I find it a welcome break from my routine work of cutting up dead bodies and searching inside for clues," he said, rising to leave.

"I may be busy in the casualty. You should leave only after taking some more rest. Anyway, the next bus for Chittar is only at five o'clock. The policemen have left with the jeep long back. I have told them to inform your hospital that you are fine." He paused at the door. "I appreciate you for the work you are doing, but I think you should be taking more care of yourself also."

It was dark by the time I reached home. I apprised Jessy of all the happenings, had supper, and got into bed. Sleep just didn't feel enough.

26. Resignation

The Vicar approached me in the OP. "Doctor, the salary revision committee has finally met and decided on your pay. They have also decided to pay the arrears of the annual leave surrender." I wondered why he was looking so apologetic and defensive. He paused for a moment. "The decision was to increase both your salaries by a hundred rupees each."

I was shocked. Last time, Zacharias Thirumeni had given an increment of ten percent- it was two hundred rupees each, and it was given exactly on time, along with the annual leave surrender."

I could not understand the basis of the committee's decision, that too, coming after such a long time. I felt insulted. I made up my mind then and there. "Please convey a meeting of the local committee urgently. I have some important announcements to make. Meanwhile, I am not claiming my arrears now. I will convey everything in the committee."

I had decided to resign and look for another job. Will my father think

I have failed him? Anyway, I should see him and explain, before a formal announcement.

I went to Thiruvalla by bus to meet him. Petrol prices had risen, and our finances were almost drained. He listened patiently to my narrative of the developments, reclining on his armchair. He was deep in thought for what seemed to be an eternity.

"It seems they are least interested in developing the hospital. At least they should have appreciated your efforts and try to retain you at whatever cost. If they are not bothered, why should you be?" He rose and walked to the dining table. "Come, lunch is ready. You will be able to take a short nap before leaving."

I was fast asleep when he woke me up at four. "Get going. Jessy might be struggling there with the kids and the hospital." I felt fresh and energized after the deep slumber that I'd forgotten was possible. All conflicts dashing across in my mind seemed to have vanished.

After the routine discussions in the meeting, I announced our decision to resign. "I am also not accepting my arrears. I am donating it to the hospital fund. I am giving a notice of three months, by which time you have to find a replacement."

All the members tried to protest, but I stood firm. "I have not yet decided on my future plans. I will try to leave only after finding a replacement," I assured them. I made sure that my notice of resignation was properly entered in the minutes of the meeting.

I put in an advertisement in the Job Wanted column of a newspaper. I also sent an application to AVT, the plantation company.

Many responses came to my ad- some even traveling from afar to meet me. The salaries offered were almost double our present pay, but they all wanted us to join within a month at least. I realized my folly of putting the advertisement so early. I had to decline all the offers, saying that I will have to wait for a replacement here before I could leave.

Another month went by and no replacement was in sight. Meanwhile, I got a letter from AVT, inviting me for an interview in Kochi. The taxi fare from my place of residence will be borne by the company. That felt good! *Even if I am not selected, I will have a free ride to Kochi and back.* And since I will be going in my own car, I will make a small profit also in the bargain!

Dr. Lonappan gave me intensive coaching for the interview. My chappals got a clear 'No!' from him. I went to buy myself a pair of shoes.

The interview was held at the corporate office of the company, by the General Manager himself. He was jovial, but at the same time, very professional. It went off well. Dr. Lonappan had given me a good background of the company and what would be their expectations from a medical officer. "We are having a vacancy for only one medical officer. Since your wife also is a qualified doctor, what will she do?" the GM asked me.

"We can find employment for her in a private hospital in Punalur, Sir," I replied.

"Will she be able to help out if some of the lady workers or the wife of a manager would like to consult a lady doctor?"

"Certainly Sir," I replied.

"Okay, we will get back to you in a month with our decision. We have a couple more applicants to interview. Don't forget to see our Accounts Officer and collect your taxi fare." *As if I would forget!*

Exactly a month on, I got a letter from the company. I had been selected! Attached was a list of my salary and other allowances and perquisites. I was to report to work within a month. I added up my emoluments and found that it would be six times what I was earning now! But there were one and a half months to go before the term of three months' notice I had given to the committee. There had been no progress in finding a new doctor. I wrote to the company asking for a two-week extension of my joining date, which was promptly agreed to.

I met the Vicar and told him of the developments. "Please wait till Valiya Thirumeni comes back," he requested. "He is on a foreign tour for three months."

"Certainly I can't wait that much. It's more than a month and a half since I have given my notice of resignation. What have you done for finding a doctor?"

"We are doing all we can, Doctor, but till now we have drawn a blank."

"Have you put an ad in the newspapers?"

"No..."

"Then what's it that you have done?" I was getting irritated. *Maybe they are thinking I will change my mind, and stay on.* "I've given you three months. Do you want the hospital to be closed again? Hope you will give the advertisement this week itself!"

The ad appeared in the Malayala Manorama newspaper the following Tuesday. My name was given as the contact person.

On Friday morning there was a doctor waiting in my room. The OP was crowded. Dr. Johnson introduced himself. "I have come, seeing your advertisement." He seemed to be already regretting the decision. "What an arduous journey, just getting here!"

Sister Mariamma popped her head in through the half door. "There is an injury, Doctor. We have applied pressure bandage, but it's still bleeding."

"Excuse me, let me see, I'll be back" I followed her into the procedure room. Sister opened the dressing for me to see. Tiny streams of blood spurted out. I put the bandage back and tightly tied it, but it soaked up, and blood was seething through it, and dripping down. I knew I had to suture it then itself. Untying the bandage, I began putting ties of thread to stop the bleeding. It took some time. I suddenly remembered Dr. Johnson who was waiting in my room.

"Ask the doctor if he can come in. We could talk while I suture this up."

Sr. Alice went to fetch the doctor.

Dr. Johnson came in and stared at the open wound, and then at the pool of blood on the floor. "Why didn't you refer this case?"

"What's the need, Doctor?" I replied. "We can manage this here. If we refuse, they will have to go all the way to Pathanamthitta, for which they should get a jeep. They will have to spend a lot."

The doctor didn't seem much to be appreciating the logic.

"This might take some time," I continued. "What about talking here while I stitch?"

"It is quite congested in here. This room should be having an AC! I'll wait in the OP room. We will talk after you finish."

Dr. Johnson seemed impatient, having waited too long. "How much will they pay?" he asked as soon as I entered.

"You will have to talk to the Vicar or Valiya Thirumeni. Right now, they are paying five thousand for me and Dr. Jessy combined."

"That's just twenty-five hundred for one doctor working full time. Are you crazy to be working here so cheap?" He looked outside to the crowd waiting. "It seems to be a very heavy OP also. I will give you my card. You can tell the management. Since I have to work alone, I will be expecting a minimum of seventy-five hundred rupees. Let them contact me only if they are willing. It seems there is no point in me wasting more time here." He left in a hurry.

I accosted the Vicar. "Why did you put me as the contact person for the applicants? Is it I who will be appointing them? And how can I answer their queries about the salary?" I gave him Dr. Johnson's card and informed him of his demand. "Anyone else who contacts, I will just refer them to you."

"Rupees seven thousand and five hundred for just one doctor? Even our Ranni hospital pays only three thousand for MBBS doctors!"

"At least now you should understand they are different," I told him rather sternly. They are duty doctors working eight hours a day and having leaves and holidays in plenty. Don't expect anyone to be on call 24/7 here, for the same salary."

As calls and enquiries came in, I directed everyone to the Vicar. By the end of the month, nobody had joined. I reminded him about the impending date. With just a week to go, he came to my room accompanied by an immaculately dressed man, approaching middle age.

"This doctor has expressed interest in joining. Please show him around the hospital and explain the work here."

Dr. Jacob Samuel seemed devoid of any real interest as I took him around. He didn't have many questions to ask me.

"Will you be coming alone?" I asked. "Will your family be accompanying you?"

"I don't have a family."

Is he still a bachelor? Could he be married and separated? I didn't ask any of the questions that came to my mind. After going through the hospital, he left with the Vicar to discuss the terms.

The Vicar met me in the evening. "We went to the Bishop's Palace in Ranny in his car. Since Valiya Thirumeni is away, we met the Vicar General who is in charge. It was decided to appoint him."

"Excellent!" I exclaimed. "Now I can leave in peace."

He did not seem to be sharing my enthusiasm. "His salary is a bit too much, Doctor. He wouldn't agree to anything less than six thousand. And he has specifically told that he will not be attending to labor cases.

I was taken aback. The salary was higher than what we were given as a couple. And if he does not attend to labor, it will mean a significant decrease in the hospital income. All those pregnant ladies coming for regular checkups will also have to go elsewhere.

The Vicar seemed to be reading my thoughts. "At least now, I hope Valiya Thirumeni will realize your worth." It was the first time I've heard the Vicar being so critical of Valiya Thirumeni.

"Anyway, it is too late," I sighed.

"Do you think the hospital will be viable without deliveries and the increase in salary expenses?"

"Of course it can be," I said confidently. "If there are no deliveries, there will always be enough beds and those patients now having to go to Pathanamthitta can be admitted here itself. But it may not be possible now to build up the hospital fund for a new building."

"There is another thing, Doctor. He wants a month's time for joining.

"Aiyo! But I have to leave in a week!"

"Please make some adjustment, Doctor. It will not be good that the hospital gets closed again for reopening after one month."

"Let me see what I can do," I said, not really sure what could possibly be done. Meanwhile, I got a letter from the Senior Manager in charge of the estate in Punalur, welcoming me. I was to report to him the following Monday. The doctor's bungalow would be kept ready. The company will pay all expenses related to my shifting.

"You go ahead," Jessy urged. "I will manage the hospital alone, till the new doctor joins."

27. Prateeksha (Hope)

Early morning next Monday, I prepared to travel to the AVT estate in Punalur. The car was packed with all my dresses and some utensils for the kitchen. I had not announced to our patients about my leaving, but many had got wind of it and came to bid me goodbye.

Sally and Johnykutty were among the crowd. "My date is just two or three weeks away. We had wished you would deliver our child." Sally was sentimental.

"Don't worry, Dr. Jessy is here. She will conduct your delivery," I assured her.

I had bid farewell to CKM the day before, but he was there to see me off. Some of my regular patients had also come. *How did they come to know that I was leaving?*

It was a two-hour drive. I took it slowly. There was a heavy feeling within me. In spite of all the stress and strain, I had loved the challenge and had become attached to many of the patients.

As I left Pathanamthitta and headed towards Punalur, my thoughts shifted to the new job. I had been instructed to go straight to the doctor's bungalow, and report to the office and meet the Senior Manager at eleven.

DG was waiting to receive me at the bungalow. As I parked the car and started unpacking, he stopped me. "Leave it. They will take care of it. Now, that is the motorcycle allotted for you." I hadn't noticed the Bullet parked inside the car shed.

He introduced me to the two youngsters with him. "This is Sekhar. He will be your butler. You are entitled to one more servant, which we will arrange by the time your family arrives. And this is Kuttappan. He is the hospital attender. He will be there for any help you need."

Kuttappan was a boyish young man, dressed in an immaculate white shirt and shorts. Sekhar was unkempt, and his cooking skills were far inferior to my own, as I was to find later.

The senior manager, Mr. Martin was a veteran planter. DG and the other assistant managers seemed to be in awe of him, but they liked him.

"Sit down, Doctor. Welcome to the estate!" He gestured to the wooden chair at the other side of his large table. I have heard about your work in Chittar, but here, your work will be quite different. I don't want you to take any risks here. You can refer any bad case to the government hospital. We will give them transportation and reimburse their expenses."

"I am used to managing somewhat bad cases, Sir," I said.

"You can get into trouble. You must understand that treatment here is free for all the workers. It is their right. The workers might not have much appreciation for your work. You have to build it up. You will learn on the way."

There was not enough work to keep me engaged. I had not seen even a single serious medical case the whole week. The majority of visitors to the hospital will be bringing some medical bills they wanted me to sign on. Others came with some minor illnesses or body aches. They wanted the strongest analgesics. Many would ask for references to specialists for simple ailments. If they had a headache, they expected me to prescribe a CT scan!

"Don't countersign any bill that you have not prescribed," Martin Sir warned me. If they say that they are regular medicines they are taking, ask them for previous records. Many would bring spurious bills. There are people who buy medicines, get it reimbursed from our office, and then sell it outside!"

"Some of them are really arrogant and persistent," I said.

"Doctor, do you know why the company is giving such a good salary and other perks to us executives?" I looked at him, not finding a proper answer. "It is so that we will suffer all the abuse and harassment from the workers for the sake of the company, while not yielding to their unreasonable demands or threats. Be fair, but firm."

The next day, DG introduced me to Jim, an assistant Manager. "He drinks like a fish, and smokes like a chimney."

"Come to my bungalow tonight. You should meet my wife. There will be the other executives of the estate. There are five of us- a separate gang, apart from the two senior Managers."

I was the first to arrive. His wife showed me some beautiful watercolor paintings she had done. I promised to teach her the basics of painting in oil.

It was a wild party. "This is a welcome party for you, but almost every day, we will have some reason to celebrate." There was dancing and singing. I was introduced to the other smart assistant and deputy managers, and their charming wives.

"When will your wife come to join?" Someone asked me.

"In a month's time, I hope," I replied. As an afterthought, I added- "but she won't touch alcohol. Not even wine!"

"Let her come. We will change all that." Jim declared confidently.

Going through the medical accounts in the office, I found that just about three percent of the employees accounted for more than eighty percent of the medical expenditure. It was no coincidence that this three per cent was mostly the labor union leaders. *Now there is something here that I have to work on.*

Saturday arrived, and I was to go to Chittar in the evening, after work. I planned to visit Jessy and the children every weekend till they join me here. I was not much worried about the petrol expenses. I was entitled to five hundred liters of petrol a year from the company. I wondered what I would do with that much petrol.

Aju and Cuckoo seemed overjoyed to see me. Jessy described how, on the day I had left, Cuckoo was crying all through the night. Finally, she had to go to the hospital well past midnight and give her some sedation. There had not been any problem in the hospital, but she had been quite busy, managing alone. I decided she needed a break.

The third week that I visited, Jessy was not at home. She was attending to a delivery at the hospital, leaving the kids with the maid. Chackochen came with a message. "Dr. Jessy asked you to come to the hospital."

Hope it's not some severe complication. I followed Chackochan. It had been three weeks since I had conducted a delivery, and already I was feeling out of touch. I was surprised to see Johnykutty, his parents, and Sally's parents gathered outside the labor room.

"It's Sally. She was asking for you," Jessy said, just as the baby's head popped out. She took hold of it and got the baby out. It was a girl, announcing her arrival into the world with a loud scream. Sally heard her wailing and smiled contentedly.

I stepped out and announced to the group outside. "It's a girl!" There were smiles all around.

Johnykutty came forward. "We are so glad that you were here today. I want to ask you for another favor. "It is our wish that you name the child."

"Okay, let me think of a name,' I said and went back into the labor room, where Jessy had already taken out the placenta, the sisters had cleaned up the baby and wrapped it up.

"Johnykutty wants me to name the baby," I told her."Any suggestions?"

"Prateeksha," she announced without hesitation. (Prateeksha in Malayalam means 'hope')

"Yes!" Sally exclaimed. "It's such a nice name."

I followed the nurse taking the baby out. Several eager hands were extended to hold the baby, but she handed the child to Johnykutty. "Prateeksha," I proclaimed.

The next day, I went to see the Vicar as soon as he came out after the church service. "When I come next week, I will be taking my family. We are leaving for good. Have you contacted Dr. Jacob? When will he be coming?"

"Yes, Doctor. Everything has been arranged. He will come by afternoon, next Sunday. I will come to the hospital on Saturday, take charge of the accounts and the balance cash. The Vicar General has asked me to handle the cash myself for the time being."

When I came home next Friday evening, Jessy and Aju were enthusiastic. I had been given leave on Saturday for the shifting. Cuckoo at just nine months of age, could not figure out the reason for our excitement. It was Jessy now who was feeling the pangs of leaving this hospital, where we had planned to spend our entire lives.

All of Saturday, I was busy packing everything in cardboard boxes, plenty of which were available from the hospital. Ceramics, glasses, my paintings, the violin, clothes, and sheets were to go in the car.

The tempo lorry arrived by noon, the next day. We were to leave by three o'clock. The loading work was done by the local head load workers, many of whom had come to us several times with their children or parents. On the rare occasions when they came for themselves, it would most often be for alcoholic gastritis.

The loading over, it was time for the payment. "We are so sad you are going away. We want to do this free for you, as a token of our gratitude," their leader told me. They were convinced to accept the money after assuring them that I would be getting reimbursement from the company.

We waited for the doctor to arrive. There were eight admitted patients still in the hospital. We had planned to take the final rounds with the new doctor and hand them over to him.

There was no sign of the doctor even after three. With all our furniture loaded in the tempo, we sat on the steps of the house, waiting for him to arrive. *What if he doesn't turn up?*

We continued to wait. The Vicar went to the hospital again to try getting him on the phone. Jessy went and sat in the car, with Cuckoo sleeping in her lap. After some time, Aju also got into the back seat and lay there. He soon fell asleep.

The Vicar was visibly anxious. "He had promised he would be here by afternoon. Nobody is picking up the phone at his house. I believe he lives alone there. What will we do if he doesn't come?" He was echoing my thoughts.

"There are eight patients here, I said. "Three of them are okay. Maybe we can send them home now itself to continue their medicines there, but the others need to be shifted to Ranni or Pathanamthitta."

By four-thirty, we decided to wait no further and went to the hospital to take the final rounds, leaving Aju and Cuckoo sleeping in the car. We explained to the patients that the new doctor has not yet arrived, and in case he doesn't turn up, they have to be transported to other hospitals. Naturally, they were very upset.

We sat down in the consultation room and wrote the prescriptions for three of them planned to be discharged and sent home. Together, we began writing detailed letters of reference for the other five. The phone rang.

It was DG from the estate office. He was waiting in the bungalow with the workers for unloading.

"The doctor supposed to take over has not turned up so far," I explained. We have to shift out the inpatients to other hospitals before we leave."

"Aiyo! It will be dark by the time you reach. Send the tempo now. We will unpack your things and set it up here."

The tempo was sent off with route directions. We completed the referral letters and returned to the house. Aju had just woken up. "When are we going?" he asked impatiently.

The Vicar was also there glancing frequently at his watch and the road. "It is nearing six o'clock. Maybe Dr. Jacob is not coming."

"We have to make arrangements to shift the patients quickly," I said. "It is our responsibility. I can't leave before that."

"Arranging five jeeps will take time, Doctor. I have a suggestion." He came up with a brilliant idea. "Can Dr. Jessy stay back for a few more days? Meanwhile, we can find out about Dr. Jacob or find someone else."

All my pent up feelings exploded. "What nonsense are you talking? All the furniture has been sent off. How can Jessy —"

I was cut off by the sight of a red Fiat approaching in a cloud of dust with a big lorry fully loaded with furniture, keeping tow.

I ran to meet Dr. Jacob. "We are late! I have to rush. We planned to take rounds together with you and handover the patients, but now we don't have the time. The children are also tired, waiting. There are eight inpatients now. We had written reference letters for all of them. You can get to know them by going through them.

"There are eight patients here now?" he exclaimed.

"It's relatively less, Doctor. Usually, there will be fifteen to seventeen."

"I might have to refer some of them. Let me see. I don't want to take too many risks. I can use the letters you have written."

I drove slowly taking care not to wake up the children, or break anything packed in the boot. Cuckoo was laid on a ledge behind the back seat of the Ambassador and Aju was sleeping on the seat.

I thought about the last three years. My dream of building up a secondary level hospital in Chittar was nowhere near achieved, but we have built up a good primary center which can take in even sick patients if the doctor is willing to take the risk. The patients had been more than willing. Childbirth has become safer. There had not been a single maternal mortality, and no infant deaths too, except for Molly's child. Many had their chronic illnesses under control and even the quacks knew how to handle common illnesses like diarrhea. Most everyone, including children, were now wearing footwear. The incidence of anemia and worm infestations has definitely come down. Many severe illnesses- children with acute nephritis, young men and women with rheumatic fever, elderly with acute respiratory and gastric illnesses, cardiac and neurological events had been managed, most of them not developing any serious complications. *Will Dr. Jacob carry it forward?*

"Will we have time there to unpack our things and cook dinner?" I was awakened from my daytime dreaming by Jessy, showing me her watch. "Should we buy something on the way?"

"Don't worry," I reassured her. "Shekhar will have cooked up something. We won't go hungry if we manage to eat it."

Sekhar and the new cook- an elderly lady called Chachamma, were there to receive us. All our furniture had been set out neatly. It seemed a bit crowded with what was there already, but the rooms were large and spacious enough to take in all.

We woke up the children. Aju wondered how he had woken up to a completely new place, but some of the furniture looked the same. By the time we washed and changed, food was served, and we sat down for dinner.

There were fluffy chapattis, delicious egg curry cooked in coconut gravy, a nicely decorated salad dressing, and mango pickle.

Epilogue

Thirty years later....

It was a Sunday, and I was still in bed. I was rudely awakened by the mobile phone ringing. The light streaming in through the window was already bright.

It was CKM!

The last time we had met was about twenty-five years ago when I was shifting to this, our ancestral house, where I have settled. He had come to help me with the shifting, along with Jim from the estate. Jessy and I now live alone here, occasionally revved up by visits from Aju and Cuckoo, both employed in distant parts of the state. Jessy looks after our own small clinic nearby and I am working as a family physician in a corporate hospital in Pathanamthitta, just six kilometers away.

CKM and I had established contact three years back when he traced my mobile number through Facebook. He has purchased and settled in a nice house in Kochi. The problem with his leg has been sorted out for good. After the death of Dr. K. M. Thomas which had left him devastated, he used to ignore the mild aches recurring in his thigh, until he had to be rushed to a high-tech hospital in Kochi in a critical condition. MRI scan revealed a tiny metal splinter lodged in his thigh bone. It might have been there for about thirty five years, undetectable in an X-ray. The culprit was removed by a young orthopedic surgeon whose age was less than that of the splinter in CKM's leg, and there had been no issues since then.

He had to sell his house and shop in Chittar to settle the medical bills, and move to a rented house in Kochi. However, he was able to return to a new job in the Gulf, and once he had saved enough, and his son became well employed there, he bought the house in Kochi. Why would he be calling me now?

"Hello, Doctor!" His voice was as bright and cheerful as ever. "Have you seen the newspapers today?"

"No... just woke up. Good thing you called. It's already late."

"Your Valiya Thirumeni is going to be felicitated nationally. He has been selected to receive the Padma Bhushan!"

"Really? He must be over a hundred now!"

"Yes, but quite healthy for his age. It is really a great honor for your church."

"Yes, and he deserves it. His oratory is unmatched and his thinking is quite broad. The best thing I like about him is that he can accommodate the views of all religions. He is certainly not tied down by dogma. I don't much care for his administrative skills though, especially after my experience with him in Chittar."

"But Doctor, if you compare him to those who have followed him in the position he held, he should be considered a saint!"

"Absolutely!" I couldn't agree more. I certainly was appalled by the unscrupulous actions of the present day men in red robes, holding supposedly holy offices.

I made myself a coffee and leaned back in my favorite armchair on the verandah. The house has been renovated in stages, and an extension built with two spacious bedrooms, though not as lavish as those in the estate.

It had been a long journey for me. Having left AVT plantations as the Group Medical Officer, I started my own clinic in our home village. Later handing over charge of our clinic to Jessy, I did freelancing- working at times in eight different hospitals at the same time, while doing vegetable and fish farming, and starting a computer center- a first in our village. I did also revisit Chittar, though as a day time consultant. *Some day, I should write a book!*

Chittar is a bustling town now. There is still no good hospital there. It is not much of a problem now, as getting to Pathanamthitta will take just thirty minutes on the smooth highway, and vehicles are available in plenty. Many owned their own cars, and buses are available every fifteen minutes.

Dr. Jacob had left after six months, and the Mission Hospital again remained closed for some time, till the church decided to give it out for rent to private doctors. There had been three or four doctors who worked for around three years each, by which time they had made enough to settle down at their home towns. Sabarimala had a full time cardiac center with two cardiologists and a cardiac ICU.

I lazily took the newspaper from the knee wall of the veranda to scan the front page. It was almost full with the results of the IAS examination and the photographs of the rank holders. The Indian Administrative Service selection exam was the one where the best young brains from all over India participated, and only a few selected. Being a Malayalam daily, it had featured a Malayalee who had secured the 12th rank, on the same page.

I flipped the page over and there was Valiya Thirumeni's handsome face, beaming broadly. The report highlighted his achievements and elaborated on how he was regarded highly by all, irrespective of region or religion. There was a separate column that gave anecdotes of his humorous retorts to tricky questions.

I saw another report about a doctor having been assaulted because an eighty-four year old man who had been admitted with stroke in his ICU, had died. *This is not news anymore!*

I was about to fold up the paper and put it away when the photograph of a clean-shaven, chubby young man caught my eye. It was in a separate box item related to the IAS results. Somehow he seemed vaguely familiar. I glanced at his name- Nazer Muhammad. I could not make any connection. A sudden flash came into my mind. His face reminded me of Sally, the young girl who had given birth to an illegitimate child in Chittar. The resemblance was uncanny.

I read through the column. The boy had secured forty-third rank in the exam. The reason he was featured prominently was the inspiring story behind his achievement. Abandoned by his parents when he was just three weeks old, he had been brought up in an orphanage in Kasargod. He excelled in his studies and the orphanage took special efforts to give him the best of education. He secured a job as a clerk in a private bank and worked for the IAS exam without any coaching. There was a statement from the Mullah who was in charge of the orphanage, praising him for his hard work, his humble and exemplary character, and high ideals.

I sat upright. I looked at the face in the photo again, and read the column once more. I rose and ran to the bedroom. Jessy was still enjoying the Sunday morning late nap. I shook her awake.

"Hey! Look at this photo," I shouted excitedly. "Can you recognize him?"

Jessy rubbed her eyes still half asleep. "Why? Who is it?"

"Read that column! And look at that photo carefully.

"I am sure about it!

"It's him! Sally's son!"

ABOUT THE AUTHOR

Dr. Thomas T. Thomas is a General Practitioner of varied experiences. He has worked in remote rural clinics, in various government Health centres, in casualty of major hospitals, and as visiting medical officer in plantations, industrial establishments and de-addiction centres. He is presently working full time as a Family Physician in Muthoot Medical Centre, Pathanamthitta.

He has multiple other interests like art, music, reading, cooking, computers, growing trees, and rearing fish. He describes himself as a Jack of all trades, though a master in none.

He now resides at his renovated ancestral house in his home village Mallassery, with his wife of more than thirty five years, Dr. Annie George, who looks after their own Family Clinic in the village. His son is an Orthopaedician married to an Ophthalmology student, and they have a cute son nearing two years of age. His daughter is working as a Judicial Officer.

How readers reviewed after reading the eBook on Kindle...

Amazon Customer - Achu Anna Mathew

A book worth reading... The writer was able to present the rural life of kerala in a very effective manner... All the incidents and characters are presented in a such a way that we feel a kind of attachment to them...

Dr. Sunil Chacko

It is a fascinating book on a rich life with multifarious experiences. TTT's insights are very valuable on the functioning of a rural hospital in what was a remote area having to deal with complex and mundane cases. Further, his efforts in rebuilding the shattered lives of Sally and Johnykutty are indeed commendable. Many congratulations on a magnificent medical and human story.

Dr. Jayasree. A.K

This is an exemplary reflection of an extra ordinary doctor pushing the boundaries of medical care beyond conventions, by being with patients empathetically in their real life situations. The writing is in unique style, witty and thought provoking. Good read for doctors and others.

Anu

A light, breezy and fast paced memoir which is heartwarming and leaves the reader wanting more. Absolutely loved the book and it was quite unputdownable

How readers reviewed after reading the eBook on Kindle...

Dr. Rajeevan K. M..

Soulful narration of own life in the guise of a story. Very honest and touching. A must read book and its paperback edition is eagerly awaited.

Preethi

This beautiful book with extremely positive vibes is crafted with simple language, subtle witty humour and a striking narrative.

It manages to send to the reader important messages without being preachy at all.

Could only be written by one who has experienced all these stories with the mind of a learner and the soul of a nurturer.

Lovely lovely book

Unputdownable and all the stories are remarkably human.

Most recommended

Chitra P.

This reminded me of the stories that my grandfather, a medical practitioner, used to narrate. It's amazing how the author has recounted varied experiences in a remote location as a doctor. Extremely well written and rich in detail. I loved the descriptions of places, of the difficulties medical procedures, the tension in the stories. Highly recommended.

How readers reviewed after reading the eBook on Kindle...

Amazon Customer

A wonderful tale about dilemma, human life and love.The character sketches are well woven and the story is interesting.A good fiction tale.

Dr. Rajeswary

When they went to Seethakuzhy,

I went along,that is what I felt.I was also poking at the abyss!.Really amazing narration.Rural life medical issues are beautifully pictured. The new generation doctors should read this book

Dr. Tony Fernandez

Lively anecdotes which makes the book interesting.

Explains many day to day problems that face a general practitioner working in remote areas.

Arun Mathew Kurien

A well woven series of short incidents that all come together in a rich but simple tapestry of words that capture your imagination and hold you in your seats. The events are all common place and believable but the author organized then in quite a good sequence that they arrest your attention. Waiting for the sequels

How readers reviewed after reading the eBook on Kindle...

Sreekumar

I found this book fascinating. It took me to Chittar and the surroundings and I loved the narrative. It is an easy to read style. The story and the way it is paced is excellent don't have to be a medical person to enjoy this book.

Beekay

Loved this book!. Excellent flow in simple yet beautiful language touching events on the life of common folks in our countryside....

Dr. Arun Kishore

...makes a very good read. Written in a simple style, with little medical jargon and in short chapters, the book describes the practice of a doctor couple in a rural part of Kerala.... In these times of fraught doctor patient relationships this book comes as a breath of fresh air.

Dr. Titus Thomas

The description is very vivid and in simple language takes his story to the masses. It clearly reminded me of the life of the great A J Cronin as is described in Adventures in Two worlds... Thomas has come out with a great book..

How readers reviewed after reading the eBook on Kindle...

Major Gen KS Venugopal

A SIMPLE, READER FRIENDLY AND CAPTIVATING BOOK. A DEDICATED DOCTOR'S LIFE AND TURBULANCES IN A REMOTE VILLAGE HOSPITAL DESCRIBED METICULOUSLY.

VK Koyilil

...The book narrates what he concentrated during his medical school days, to equip himself well to serve in rural areas. How he navigated professionally, clearing all obstacles and ultimately how he won the hearts of the public makes it a fantastic story...

Dinesh.M

... Written in a simple endearing style, every chapter of the book is packed with its share of human emotions... The author has soaked his life time experience in the community in every page of this book carefully dissecting the human bondage and sufferings.Like Albert Camus once wrote 'who taught you all this doctor'; the answer "Suffering".Dr.Thomas T Thomas embodies that spirit and he live it in every page if this book.

Amazon Customer

Thoroughly enjoyed reading this book. Brilliantly descriptive, easy - going language makes the stories come alive...

Printed in Great Britain
by Amazon